MARRYING THE MIDWIFE

BELOW THE SALT SERIES
BOOK TEN

ELIZABETH ROSE

OLIVERHEBERBOOKS

AUTHOR'S NOTE

My Below the Salt Series is a second generation romance stemming from my **Legacy of the Blade Series.**

There is a family tree at the back of the book in the *From the Author* section if you would like to see the relationships of the characters in both the *Legacy of the Blade* and the *Below the Salt* series.

PROLOGUE
ENGLAND, 1372

Margaret Whitlock, known as Maggie by her friends and family, made her way up the steep staircase of Ashenden Castle, extremely fatigued and finding it hard to breathe. She gripped fresh towels under one arm while holding tightly to the rope secured along the stone wall with her other hand. These twisting staircases were not only steep, but very narrow. And treacherous. Maggie couldn't risk a fall. Especially not in her condition.

As her mother's assistant, Maggie had been learning the trade of midwife all her life. Helping to birth babies came naturally to her now, and she was more than ready to go off on her own. Even though she was only six-and-ten years of age and much younger than most girls occupying this position, she still had the skills as well as the confidence of a much older, experienced midwife.

Today, Lady Anora Bohun of Ashenden was giving birth in the west tower. Maggie could hear the woman's cries of pain from the room at the top of the stairs. Assisting with births was nothing new for Maggie. She'd been present at the births of hundreds of babies of servants, townsfolk, and even nobles, ever since she was the precious age of six. Her mother, Margaret, whom Maggie was named after, was known throughout the land as one of the best and most sought-after midwives. Maggie was also her mother's only daughter. It was evident that she would one day take up the trade, following in her mother's footsteps like all of her ancestors had done before her.

Even after the death of Maggie's father three years ago, her mother remained strong, and carried on to raise and support two children on her own. Aye, the woman's talents were revered by all, especially the nobles of the land. Never had Maggie's mother lost a single baby through the years, and that was not an easy feat to claim.

Far too many children were lost at birth, a truth that deeply saddened her. And even if a babe survived birth, a good share of them died before completing their first year. Others might get through childhood, only to perish before becoming an adult. Because of this, Maggie's mother's skills had earned her good pay as well as an honorable reputation. Even if she was naught but a commoner. Her good luck, Maggie was sure, was because of the quartz crystal pendant her mother wore on a cord around her neck, that had been Maggie's grandmother's at one time.

Anxiety filled Maggie as she looked down to that same lucky crystal hanging from a cord around her neck right now. Her mother had been woken in the middle of the night and summoned to the castle. She'd left in a hurry, not even taking her lucky charm with her. She'd been letting Maggie wear it at home, insisting it would bring health and good luck to both Maggie and her unborn child. Her mother instructed her to stay in bed, but Maggie would hear none of it. Instead, she'd hurried after her to help her. She only hoped she wasn't too late, since she'd stopped at the washwoman's hut for clean towels, knowing her mother would have had no time to do so.

The door to the tower room at the top of the stairs squeaked open. "Oh, Maggie, it is ye," said Lady Anora's handmaid, looking as if she were about to go somewhere, but stopping when she saw Maggie.

"Yes, I brought towels," Maggie explained.

"Hurry, please," begged the troubled chambermaid. "Your mother is in dire need of those towels. My lady is bleeding heavily. I fear that something is very wrong indeed." The chambermaid disappeared again behind the closed door.

"Oh, nay!" cried Maggie, stopping in her tracks at hearing the disturbing news. The rapid beating of her heart made her entire chest hurt. If the noblewoman's baby didn't survive, this could mean trouble for her mother. If the baby and the noblewoman both died, her mother might end up being imprisoned, or even worse, executed. Even if the fault wasn't that of the midwife, it was she who would be blamed in the end. Nobles didn't take kindly to these types of situations, and neither did they forgive easily. Maggie had to give help! Her mother needed her. She would not abandon her at a trying time like this.

Even though she did her best to hurry, Maggie's own very pregnant belly weighed her down, keeping her from moving as quickly as she'd have liked to. In her alarmed state, her inner gut warned her that she needed to be cautious and put her own baby's safety above all else. Still, she had to continue because Lady Anora was in trouble. Not to mention, Maggie's mother didn't have her lucky charm with her. Clutching the fresh towels, Maggie made it to the top of the stairs, waddling over and pushing open the door to the tower room, following the trail of the handmaid.

"Oooooh! Aaaaah!" groaned the noblewoman in pain, sitting on the birthing chair that was used by women in labor. She was a shrewd wench with squinty eyes and a pointy chin. Her black hair was pulled upward, so taut that it made the white skin of her face seem overly stretched. The woman's gown was pushed up to her knees and her undergarments had been removed in preparation of the birth.

Lady Anora's daughter, Beatrice, who was the same age as Maggie, watched in silence from the other side of the room. Three handmaids were in the room to assist with the birth. Lady Anora was too old to be having a baby, already having a sixteen-year-old daughter. This was always risky when a woman who was past her prime tried to birth a baby. The noblewoman leaned back on the chair, her handmaid supporting her body from behind. A cut-out in the seat of the chair was there for the midwife to work and grab the baby and guide it as it emerged.

Maggie's mother Margaret was seated in front of the lady of the castle, her hands already in position. The midwife tools, which included scissors, trays, baskets, thread, and many linen wraps, were on a small table at her side. So were her mother's healing balms and creams, made from herbs they had grown in their garden or collected together out in nature. Her mother wore the normal midwife coverings, consisting of a long white apron over her simple wool gown, and a small white cap that covered her braided hair.

"I'm here, Mother," announced Maggie, her hand going to the crystal, rubbing it between her fingers the way she'd been doing for the past few weeks now.

"Finally," snapped the noblewoman's daughter. "You deliberately dragged your feet in getting here."

"Nay, I hurried as fast as I could." Maggie tried to defend herself to the horribly arrogant and mean girl. Suddenly, Maggie felt a gush of water at her feet and looked down to see her gown soaked. Her stomach clenched and heat engulfed her. This couldn't be happening right now! Feeling the bile rising in her throat, Maggie pushed the clean towels into the chambermaid's hands, grabbing a nearby empty wooden bowl and retching into it.

"How dare you get sick in my mother's bedchamber," said the arrogant Beatrice with her nose in the air.

"Maggie!" Maggie's mother looked up in surprise and concern. "Why are you here? I told you to stay home today. You shouldn't have come and neither should you have climbed the stairs in your condition. What were you thinking?"

"I'm here to assist you, Mother. Like I always do." Maggie released a loud groan of pain and became dizzy, almost falling over.

Her mother shot to her feet and ran over to help her sit on a wooden stool. "Let me take a look at you," said her mother, pushing up Maggie's gown and frowning. "Your water has broken. You are in labor and your baby is coming fast."

"Nay," mumbled Maggie, shaking her head in denial. "It

can't be. Not now, not here." This couldn't be happening to her. It shouldn't be happening. Things just kept getting worse this night.

"Midwife! Get back over here," shouted the noblewoman's daughter. "My mother's baby is all that will take your concern now. Leave that common girl be. She is not important."

"But Maggie is my daughter and she is in labor too," Maggie's mother told Beatrice.

"Are you denying to help me?" Lady Anora's daggered gaze rained down on them now, causing the servants in the room to cower in fear. Beatrice strutted over to her mother, placing her hand on the woman's shoulder.

"Don't worry, Mother. If they disobey, I will be sure to make them suffer."

When Maggie saw the turmoil on her mother's face, she realized this was a bad situation and it was all her fault. Maggie's mother had told her to stay in bed, and now she realized she should have listened to her. She'd made a big mistake by coming here tonight. Staying in their cottage with the neighbor women watching after her would have been a wise thing to do, because climbing the steep staircase had brought the beginning of the arrival of her baby. It wasn't time for this yet. Nay. It was happening much too soon!

Her mother glanced at the noblewoman and then back at Maggie.

"Go, Mother," Maggie whispered, feeling frightened for the first time in her life. She was scared not only for her own baby's fate, but because Lady Anora was bleeding profusely and her baby seemed to be caught in the birth canal. Also, because Beatrice was threatening them. "Help Lady Anora, Mother. Take your lucky charm from me." Her hand went to the necklace. "You need it to—oh nay," she cried, stopping suddenly as she felt her own babe starting to emerge.

"I won't leave you, Maggie." Her mother looked down, trying to help Maggie's babe be born. The pain Maggie felt was so intense that she wanted to die. Tears filled her eyes.

"Midwife, please," begged the chambermaid wringing her hands together. "My lady and her baby are in peril. Ye must tend to the noblewoman first. It is your duty."

"The king and our laws will it so," screamed Beatrice. "Get back to work, now!"

Maggie tried to hold back her screams of pain by biting the inside of her cheek until it bled. This was Lady Anora's chamber and she was a commoner who should be silent and half-hidden in the shadows. The last thing she wanted to do was to take attention away from a noble.

The room filled with wails from Lady Anora now, and blood flowed like a river. The extra towels Maggie had brought with her were already soaking wet. Maggie looked down to see that she was bleeding as well. The thought hit her hard that she might die birthing her baby tonight, along with the noblewoman. It was too horrific of a situation to accept. All Maggie had ever wanted since she was a child was to be a mother someday. Having her own baby was her dream. This meant the world to her and she refused to die and lose her child tonight. Nay, she would not give up. "Don't let me die, Mother!" wailed Maggie, frantically clutching her mother's arm with one hand and the crystal that was resting against her chest with her other hand.

Margaret Whitlock was experienced and usually knew

how to hide any worries or concerns. However, tonight Maggie witnessed distress on her mother's face.

"I won't let anything happen to you, sweetheart," her mother told her, with a kind smile that didn't light up her eyes in the least. Instead she looked tired and spent. "I promise I won't abandon you. Ever."

"You will leave that common wench and come here immediately, midwife, or I swear I will have your head," threatened Lady Anora, wincing in pain. The maids in the room rushed around in a frenzy, not sure what to do or who to help first.

"You heard my mother," squawked Beatrice. "Get over here and help her right now! Leave that pitiful girl because she doesn't matter in the least."

Her mother's eyes filled with tears. It was obvious she knew what was required of her—

however she still didn't know what to do. She had the choice to help the noblewoman or to help Maggie. She couldn't do both at the same time.

"Go, Mother." Maggie gave her the permission she needed, huffing and puffing with her heavy breathing, feeling as if she were about to swoon. Her mother's fate hung in the balance and Maggie couldn't let her suffer because of Maggie's own thoughtless actions. "The noblewoman and her baby are more important. You have a duty to them."

"Nay, Maggie, that is not true. You and my unborn grandchild are more important to me," said her mother under her breath. "You are my daughter. My only daughter, and the reason for everything I do." With the next scream of the noblewoman, her mother glanced over her shoulder once more shaking her head. Beatrice started to scream at her. "I'll be right back," she promised. She jumped up, snatching a towel from a handmaid and wiping the blood from her hands before positioning herself once again between the knees of the noble. "Handmaid, help my daughter. Please," she called out, before letting Lady Anora once again take her attention. "Push, push!" screamed Maggie's mother, but the noblewoman was too haughty and lazy to want to do anything for herself.

"Nay, I can't push. You will pull the damned thing out. Get it out of me right now!" commanded the woman, as if she thought it was really that easy.

"It is your job, midwife," snapped Beatrice. "Do what my mother says, I command you. If not, you will be punished severely."

Maggie felt so much pain now that she could no longer hold back her screams. She fell off the stool to the floor, knowing her baby was coming fast and that there was nothing she could do to slow it down. Not able to birth it herself, she wished that she could, in order to allow her mother the time needed for her to give the noble her undivided attention.

"Something is wrong," shouted the handmaid with widened eyes, helpless as she watched the birthing of Maggie's baby. "I don't think it should look like this, should it?"

"Maggie, I'm coming." Her mother threw down the towel and ran to Maggie to see what was happening. "It's all right," she assured her daughter, relief washing over her face. "The babe is just being born face up, but at least it is not breech. Push, Daughter. Push hard. I know it isn't easy, but you've got to help your child come into this world."

Maggie did as instructed. With her mother's help, her baby was born quickly with no complications under her mother's excellent care. Through tear-filled eyes Maggie saw her mother cut the cord extending from the baby to the womb. Then her mother momentarily cradled her newborn grandchild in her arms, smiling down in love and admiration.

"Congratulations, Maggie. You now have a daughter of your own. And I have my first grandchild." Pride beamed in the woman's eyes. "She is perfect in every way."

The noblewoman screamed again from the other side of the room, the pain too much for her to bear. Maggie's mother quickly wrapped the baby in a birthing blanket and handed the little girl to Maggie. When Maggie's eyes fell upon her daughter, she forgot all her pain and worries. Joy filled her being, and life seemed good again. Her daughter truly was the most perfect baby she had ever seen or held in her life. A few bright blonde, wispy curls graced her child's head. A cute little button nose and sweet heart-shaped lips mesmerized Maggie, making her unable to look away. Then, to her surprise, the little baby's eyes drifted open though she was only a newborn. Dark brown eyes, like the baby's dear departed father, were a surprise, but a memory that would live on in Maggie's mind forever from her late husband.

Maggie's happiness of her newborn was soon diminished when she noticed her mother send one of the handmaids from the room. Beatrice glared at her from her own mother's side. Then Maggie's mother came over to her with a look of horror washing over her face. Usually experienced with hiding her emotions, this surprised Maggie. There was no doubt in her mind that something terrible was about to happen. Her mother actually looked frantic. And scared.

"What is it, Mother? What's wrong? Why did you send the handmaid from the room?" asked Maggie, still cradling her baby in her arms, holding the little frail girl against the warmth of her own chest.

"I sent her to fetch Lord Florian," she said, speaking of the noblewoman's husband.

"Why?" asked Maggie. "Men are not allowed in the room when a birth is taking place."

Her mother hunkered down next to her, speaking in hushed tones so only Maggie could hear. "Listen to me closely, Maggie. Take your baby and leave here quickly." Her gaze flashed over to the nobles and then back to Maggie.

"What?" Maggie looked up and blinked several times in succession. "Whatever for?"

"Lady Anora's baby is stuck in the birth canal and I am having a hard time removing it. Unfortunately, the child has the cord wrapped around its neck. Also, it is not moving at all and is not breathing. I'm afraid I am too late. The poor baby is already dead even though it is yet to be born. I will baptize it, but there is no hope that it will live. Lady Anora has also lost so much blood that I fear she might not survive the night either. That is why I sent for her husband."

A midwife was authorized to baptize a baby if it was a stillborn or died just after birth. Maggie knew this. However, she had never seen it happen before. Never in the past had her mother had such ill luck fall upon her as she did tonight.

"They might both die? Mother, nay," Maggie whispered

back, not wanting the evil Beatrice to hear their conversation. Her heart lodged in her throat. "If that happens, you will be blamed and imprisoned in the dungeon. Or possibly executed."

"I know," said her mother, tears streaming down her cheeks. She reached out and caressed the head of Maggie's newborn, giving it one last gentle look. Then she cupped Maggie's cheek in her blood-stained hand. "Take your brother and flee this town and never look back, do you understand?"

"Nay, I don't."

"I don't want them to come for you as well," her mother continued. "You are a mother now, with a newborn daughter, Maggie. You need to give the child the best chance of having a normal life. Plus, Charles is still young and needs someone to watch over him. Don't let the dark shadow of what happens here tonight hang over your head. You need to flee and live the good life you deserve."

"Nay, Mother, don't say that. I'll never abandon you." She reached for the crystal pendant. "You just need your lucky charm, that's all."

"Nay." Her mother's hand clamped down over Maggie's, keeping her from removing the necklace. "My good luck has run out. Nothing can change the events of this awful evening. The charm is yours now, Daughter. Mayhap it will bring good luck to you and your newborn instead."

"Mother, I'm not leaving you," said Maggie stubbornly, not knowing what she could possibly do to help, but not wanting to abandon her mother in her time of need.

"You must go. Do it now, and don't fight me about this." Her mother's voice was strong and stern.

"Midwife, get over here!" screamed Beatrice.

"I can't and won't leave you. You are family," said Maggie, knowing family was the most important thing in life.

"Find a new family," said her mother. "You must. It is time. You will need a father for your daughter so she doesn't grow up without one the way you and Charles have had to do for the past few years."

Maggie didn't know what to say. Neither could she continue to speak because she felt too choked to even try. Her mother helped her to her feet as the newborn baby started to wail, pushing a small pouch of coins into Maggie's hand. Clutching her crying baby to her chest, Maggie wondered if somehow her newborn understood what was happening here and felt the sorrow as well.

"Handmaid, go with my daughter and help her get down the stairs and back to the cottage safely," instructed her mother to a second handmaid that was present. "My daughter will pay you handsomely once she arrives safely at home." She looked back at Maggie and reached down to kiss the little baby on the head. Then she kissed Maggie on the cheek. "Goodbye, Maggie. Take good care of the baby and your brother. I love you all, so please remind them of it every day."

With another scream from the noblewoman and Beatrice spouting more evil threats, Maggie's mother turned and hurried back to work.

Maggie cried hard, struggling to walk to the door, having just given birth and feeling weak, drained and very shaky. She decided to let the handmaid carry her newborn daughter for fear that she might drop the poor child. Once at the door, Maggie glanced back over her shoulder to see her mother birthing a blue, lifeless baby with the umbilical cord around its neck, just as her mother had predicted. It was a boy. Sure enough, Lady Anora's child was a stillborn. When the noblewoman saw her baby she fainted. Beatrice screamed and started threatening Maggie's mother once again.

"I love you, Mother," cried Maggie, seeing her mother turn toward her with pain and despair on her face.

"Goodbye, Maggie," her mother called out. "And remember, never, *ever* look back. You need to move forward now and carry on with your life. Now go!" Her mother nodded to the handmaid who guided Maggie from the room. A third maid hurried over and closed the door behind them.

Today should have been the happiest day of Maggie's life, but instead it turned into the most dreadful, horrible day ever. She wished she could do it all over again, because if she had stayed at the cottage like her mother had instructed, things might be different right now. If so, her mother might have been able to focus solely on the noblewoman's baby instead of Maggie's. Mayhap then she could have saved the noble's baby, after all.

This was all her fault, Maggie decided. Without meaning to, she'd made her mother choose between saving her baby or the noble's child. What her mother did, she did out of love. But that love was also the deciding factor of her mother's doomed fate. Now, because of that undying love, Maggie realized she would never see her mother alive again.

Maggie swore that she'd never forgive herself as long as she lived.

When they arrived at the cottage, Maggie paid the hand-maid and hurriedly started to pack whatever she could carry.

"Charles," she told her nine-year-old brother. "Help me pack our things. We need to leave at once."

"Where is Mother?" asked the boy.

"She's not coming with us," said Maggie, trying to stay strong so her brother wouldn't be frightened. Her baby started crying. She made a sling out of a blanket and tied the baby to her chest.

"Is that your baby, Maggie?" asked the boy.

"Yes, this is my daughter. Now, hurry up and pack. We are leaving and never going to return."

"Why not?" asked Charles, doing as she told him.

"Because, it is what Mother wants."

"I don't understand," whined the boy. "Where is Mother? I want her to come with us."

"Just do what I say and don't ask questions." Maggie hated being so stern with her brother, but there was no time to explain things now.

A knock came at the door and Maggie ran over to open it. It was her neighbor, Gertrude. The woman worked at the alehouse and was her mother's best friend. She looked to be crying.

"What is it, Gertrude? Why are you so upset?"

"Oh, Maggie, I heard what happened. They are going to execute your mother."

Maggie felt dizzy and as if she were going to swoon. "Do you know this for sure?"

"Yes, I saw the guards pulling her across the courtyard to the dungeon. She was in chains," wailed the woman.

"Oh, Gertrude, we need to do something to help her."

"Nay, you mustn't go back to the castle," warned Gertrude. "I heard the guards are looking for you and your baby as well. Lady Beatrice told them that Lady Anora and her baby both died because your mother helped you to birth your baby instead. They are going to execute your mother and then come and do the same to you and your child. Lord Florian has already given the command."

"Please tell me this isn't so, Gertrude!"

"I'm afraid it's the truth," she cried. "The nobles are blaming you and your baby for the deaths today. They say that it is only fair that both you and your daughter die as well, to right the wrong that has been committed."

Fear coursed through Maggie as her baby continued to cry. She held the child tightly against her to try to calm her. She ran over and put her arm around Charles and hugged him to her side. "I don't know where to go or what to do," said Maggie, her body shaking like a leaf in the wind.

"My husband has a horse and wagon waiting. You and Charles and your daughter can hide in the back in the hay. He'll take you as far as the next town, but you'll be on your own after that. I'm sorry."

"Nay, it's too dangerous for Harold to risk his life to help us. I don't want either of you punished because of me."

"Maggie," said the woman, taking her hands in hers. "Your mother delivered all my children and saved my youngest when it didn't look like he would survive. I owe her this. You are all like family to me. I can never repay her for everything she's done. If I can help you escape the same awful fate as her own, then I know she will have been thankful to me."

"All right," said Maggie, knowing since she'd just given birth that she'd never be able to walk fast or far or even ride a horse. She needed to take whatever help was offered. "I will go. I will do it for my baby and for Charles. But I really wish I could do something to save my mother."

The bells in the castle courtyard started ringing in that certain way they always did when there was about to be an execution.

"It's Mother, isn't it?" she asked in a whisper. "They're going to hang her or behead her with everyone watching." Maggie was too terrified even to cry.

"I'm afraid so," said Gertrude.

"I want to go to her. I have to be there with her when she loses her life. I won't abandon her."

"Nay," said Gertrude, shaking her head adamantly. "Your cannot do a thing to stop it and your mother would never forgive me if I let you children watch her execution. Now go! Harold is waiting with the horse and cart. He will take you three to safety but you must leave right now. The guards will come looking for you soon."

"Thank you, Gertrude," said Maggie, giving the woman a hug. She picked up some of their belongings. "Bring whatever you can carry, Charles, but we need to leave right now."

Charles left the cottage following Gertrude. Maggie stopped in the doorway to look back once more at the place that had been her home for her entire life. The fire still burned on the hearth and there were remnants of a last meal still on the table. Most of their belongings were going to have to be left behind. It pained her to do so. Her late father had carved the spindly legs of their eating table, as well as the birds and trees on the back of the chairs. Her mother always loved this table and chairs, and said they were her only and last remembrance of her beloved husband. The curtains blowing in the breeze on the windows were each embroidered by her mother's hand. On each curtain her mother had sewed the names of the babies she had delivered throughout the years. Maggie didn't even have a name for her daughter yet. She had so been looking forward to having her child's name added to the rest of the babies that her mother had a hand in bringing into this world.

So many memories. Such a happy life. But now those memories would be naught but dreams, overshadowed by the new nightmare that weighed heavy on her mind. Maggie realized she would never be able to return here but neither did she want to, since Ashenden would only hold sorrow, grief, and horror for her from this day on.

CHAPTER I

FOUR YEARS LATER, SALTWOOD CASTLE, HYTHE

Today was the day that Lord Evan Blackmore would finally be knighted, and he couldn't be any happier. The satisfying feeling of true pride expanded his chest. Now he was following in the footsteps of his respected father, Lord Garrett Blackmore, who was also a knight, not to mention the king's Lord Warden of the Cinque Ports.

Standing next to Evan was his cousin, Daegel Blake. Both of them were dressed in long white tunics that depicted purity, truth, and loyalty. Over their tunics and hose they wore red cloaks. The red color symbolized sacrifice, the blood of the battle, and valor.

They'd spent the night praying in the chapel of Saltwood Castle, after having first bathed and cleansed themselves of their sins. This needed to be done before taking their knightly vows. They'd been required to place their swords atop the altar, while they prayed and asked for God's forgiveness and his blessing during this important and special time. They'd been locked in the room together all night, neither of them getting any sleep. But this morning the doors were opened by Brother Ruford, who was Daegel's uncle. The monk was joining them today to conduct the dubbing ceremony alongside the bishop. King Edward III should have been the one to give them the accolades, since Evan was a son of the king's Lord Warden. Unfortunately, King Edward was deathly ill, and couldn't even get out of bed.

"It is time," announced Ruford, in a soft and gentle voice. He was a short, round man who liked to eat. He usually had a cheery disposition. "I will retrieve your swords from the altar and follow you to the outdoor dais when the ceremony will be conducted. Your sponsors are already waiting there for you. So is everyone from the castle, the servants, and all the townsfolk, too."

This was already proving to be a huge celebration today. Both Evan and Daegel's fathers barred no expense with preparations, and opted to invite everyone, as well as feed all the people with an elaborate feast afterward. The onlookers were also asked to join in the excitement of viewing the joust that immediately followed the knighting ceremony.

The men slowly made their way out of the castle and across the courtyard to the raised platform where the cere-mony would take place. Atop the dais was a small altar where the Bishop of Hythe stood silently waiting. with his hands folded in prayer. Dressed in long white robes and a tall mitre, or hat, the bishop looked overly tall and saintly, or perhaps even angelic.

The crowd in the courtyard watched in silent awe with wide eyes, not wanting to miss a thing. This was an honorable ceremony, and they all cherished the fact they'd been invited to be there.

Garrett Blackmore, Evan's father, would be his sponsor today. Daegel's father, Lord Corbett Blake, would serve as Daegel's benefactor.

This June day was thankfully dry and warm, with no threats of rain to ruin the celebration. The sun shone strongly overhead, warming the air. There was not a cloud in the sky and only a slight and gentle breeze. The strong scent of cinnamon and spice drifted from the kitchen to the courtyard in the summer air.

Evan nodded to the nobles as he walked, smiling fondly as he passed the servants as well as the merchants, craftsmen, and commoners from the nearby town. He wanted to think they all cared enough about him to want to be there for him today, but in reality he realized they were probably only there because they didn't want to miss out on a free meal and a tankard of ale.

"This is it, Cousin," Daegel whispered from directly behind him. "We're actually about to become knights. Can you believe it?"

"Quit talking so much," mumbled Evan, not bothering to even look at Daegel, since his cousin was much too excited about this, and in his opinion often acted too immature.

Both Daegel and Evan were twenty-one years of age. It was the age when a nobleman was usually knighted. At seven years old, they'd served as pages. At fourteen, they'd moved on to being squires for other knights. Their training consisted of learning to use weapons to fight, protecting their lord, jousting, learning the codes of chivalry, and even exposure to courtly etiquette that included music and something Evan never care for—dancing. They both more than possessed the skills needed to become an honorable knight. Evan was quicker than his cousin with a blade in his hand; however, Daegel tended to outshine him when it came to the joust. Either way, it didn't matter. After today, they'd both go from being lords to 'sirs,' and their lives would change considerably for the better.

They ascended the stairs with Evan leading the way. Once atop the platform, Evan looked down at the crowd, feeling choked with emotion. Becoming a knight meant everything to him. He wanted to make his father and mother proud. This was the first step. Next, he'd be betrothed to marry a noblewoman for the purpose of alliances. Hopefully he and his bride would quickly have an heir and possibly at least six sons to follow in his footsteps. Every knight wanted sons, and many of them. Evan was no exception.

His sister Eleanor's red hair caught his eye from the scores of people watching from below. Eleanor stood at the foot of the dais with their mother, Echo, on one side and her husband, Connor, on the other. Connor cradled their six-month-old daughter, Elizabeth, in his arms. Evan's cousin, Edgar, or Gar, who had been raised as his brother, was right behind Eleanor, holding the hand of his wife, Josefina. In the crook of Gar's muscular arm was nestled their six-month-old baby boy, Eliot. It seemed that using the letter E for names ran rampant in his family. He'd have to come up with more E names to add to the tradition, once he had children of his own.

Brother Ruford followed them up the steps, still holding their swords. The monk took his place next to the bishop.

"Shall we start?" asked the bishop, raising his hands in prayer. Everyone gave the bishop their attention as the holy man spoke of what was to be expected of the men being knighted today, and what a responsibility as well as an honor it was to not only serve the king, but to be called Sir.

"Bring forth the swords, please," instructed the bishop. Ruford held out the men's swords for the bishop to bless them one at a time. The sponsors then girded the sheaths for the swords around Evan and Daegel's waists. Next, they helped to don them in their armor, also attaching their new spurs that were a sign of being a knight.

"Please kneel in front of your sponsors," instructed the bishop.

Once they did, their sponsors had them say their vows.

"Do you promise to always serve God, the church, your king, and your liege lords?" asked Corbett.

"I do," replied Evan and Daegel.

"Do you promise to protect the weak and defenseless, as well as to give succor to widows and orphans?" asked Garrett.

"I do," they answered together.

The vows that continued included never turning their back on a foe, never attacking an unarmed man, and never refusing a challenge from an equal. They also promised to live by honor and for glory.

Brother Ruford handed the swords to the sponsors. Evan's father held out the weapon for Evan to kiss the flat side of his blade. Daegel followed suit.

"Remember to always be loyal, true, and trustworthy to God and to your people," Corbett reminded them.

"You will serve them both now," added Garrett. "The duality is symbolized by the two edges of your blade."

"Remember to always give to the poor and to help those in need," both Garrett and Corbett said together, ending this part of the ceremony.

Then Evan's father took the sword, and using the flat end, touched first one of Evan's shoulders and then the other. "I dub you, Sir Evan," said Garrett. "Please stand."

When both Evan and Daegel had received their accolades and stood, their sponsors handed them their new and shiny helms.

The crowd cheered wildly as the sound of the long trumpets filled the air, announcing the end of the ceremony.

"Squires, bring forth our new knights' shields, lances, and horses," commanded Garrett. The two boys who would now be squires to Evan and Daegel came forth with the equipment as told. "Everyone will now head to the lists, where our new knights will partake in the joust," Garrett continued. "The joust will be followed by a grand feast right here in the courtyard to celebrate our new knights, Sir Evan Blackmore and Sir Daegel Blake. Everyone is gratefully invited."

Cheers went up again from the crowd. Children began to run around and several dogs started barking.

"Sir Evan, Sir Daegel," said Corbett in a loud voice. "It is time to go to your horses and partake in the joust."

"Congratulations," said Evan's father, reaching over and kissing Evan on the cheek as was custom. Corbett did the same to Daegel. More excitement and lots of noise came from the crowd, making Evan proud that he was now an honored knight. He slapped the helm over his head and headed down the stairs.

"Charles, where is Emma?" Maggie panicked, seeing that her thirteen-year-old brother no longer held the hand of her four-year-old daughter. The crowd inside the courtyard of Saltwood Castle started pushing, eager to get to the lists to watch the new knights joust. Maggie worried, since a little girl could easily get crushed.

"I don't know." Charles brushed his long blond bangs out of his eyes. "She was here just a minute ago."

"You were supposed to be watching her!" Maggie snapped, moving to her other arm her basket that held her instruments of being a midwife. She and her brother had been taking turns carrying Emma when she got tired. On Maggie's back were some of their belongings wrapped in a blanket and held around her by a large knot. Charles carried two oversized travel bags that held clothes and bedding. The food that had been in there keeping them from starving was long gone.

"I'm too tired from walking and too hungry to even think straight," complained her brother.

"Well, look for her! Quickly. Emma! Emma!" cried Maggie, pushing her way through the rowdy crowd.

They had spent the last two days walking here from Arborfield after having to leave their temporary home because of lack of work. With no father since they were young, and after the death of their mother four years ago, Maggie had to raise and support Emma and Charles on her own. They moved from place to place often, mainly for their own safety. It was a hard way to live, but Maggie needed to keep her family on the move. Even after four years, she feared the guards at Ashenden might be trying to find her.

They'd stopped in many towns on the way here, hoping to find work for her along the way. Sadly, each town already had an established midwife, and Maggie's skills were not needed nor wanted. Maggie longed for a permanent home, but was sure they would never have one. Charles was old enough now to be helping bring in an income, but sadly Maggie never had the time to teach him a skill. Both Charles and Emma were more or less loners, because they never stayed in one place long enough for them to make friends.

They'd approached Hythe this morning, hoping for the best. They were out of food and money, and Maggie prayed for help in finding them their next meal and a place to lay their heads. That's when they saw groups of villagers and commoners all heading to the castle. When she'd asked where they were going, she'd been told there was a knighting happening today at Saltwood Castle for Lord Daegel of Steepleton and the Lord Warden's son, Lord Evan. Everyone was invited to join in the celebration and also to attend the feast. Charles had heard this and begged her to let them go. Desperately needing food and wishing to find work, Maggie wholeheartedly agreed.

"Emma!" shouted Maggie, spying her young daughter just up ahead. The little girl was crying and rubbing her eyes, not looking where she was going. "Let me through!

Move aside, please. I need to get to my daughter." Maggie fought the crowd, pushing her way closer to little Emma. No one was listening to her and quickly once again her path was blocked. The people were all shouting and cheering and waving their hands in the air. Strolling minstrels passed by her plucking lutes, and one banged loudly on a naker, or drum. A juggler tossed balls in the air, catching them with his eyes to the sky as he danced through the crowd. One ball came so close that it almost hit her on the head.

Finally, she managed to break through the crowd, hauling her belongings with her, trying to keep dirty, raggedly dressed children and seedy-looking men from trying to steal from her. Maggie's muscles ached, creating spasms of which she could not control. Her feet felt swollen and her shoes had holes in them so large that she could actually see her toes.

"There she is," she said to herself, once again getting a glimpse of her daughter. But before she could get to Emma, a knight with a helm atop his head bounded down the stairs of the raised platform, barreling into the little girl and knocking her to the ground.

"Emma!" screamed Maggie, running to her daughter who was sitting in a mud puddle bawling.

"Whoa, there," said the knight, realizing just what happened. He stopped in his tracks and lifted his visor, looking to the ground. "Get out of my way, little girl. You're going to get hurt."

The man's insolence infuriated Maggie. She placed her basket on the ground and scooped up her crying daughter, holding her against her chest. "Mayhap you are the one who should watch where you're going," she spat. "My daughter is only four. She was lost and scared." She glared at the knight as she rubbed her daughters back, not caring that the little girl's muddied dress was soiling her clothes as well.

The crowd around her settled down. Seeing the knight, some of the people stepped back as if they were expecting trouble. Mayhap she shouldn't have spoken this way to a noble, but she was too tired and hungry and frustrated to even care. Her daughter was in danger and as her mother, Maggie would stop at nothing to protect her.

"What did you say?" The knight turned his head to look at Maggie now. Through the slats on his visor he peered out at her, perusing her with bright green eyes. Those eyes were much too alluring for such a haughty, arrogant man.

"You heard me," she said, her gaze lowering as her confidence started to waver. She'd heard gasps and whispers from behind her, making her start to rethink things because of the crowd's reaction.

"What is that foolish girl doing?" a woman asked her husband. "Lord Evan is a knight. She cannot speak to him that way."

"She'll get what's coming to her," the man replied to his wife. "No noble will allow a commoner to talk to him like that. She'll be punished for sure."

Maggie's stomach twisted into a knot. She was already down on her luck and didn't need to be imprisoned or fined because of how she just spoke to a lord, only trying to protect her daughter. If she was taken away from Charles and Emma, they surely wouldn't survive.

"I—I'm sorry, my lord, but you knocked into my daughter and I was afraid she was hurt." Emma continued to cry.

"Evan, what's going on? Why did you stop?" A second knight wearing a helm came up behind the first. "Our squires are waiting with our horses. Everyone is anxious to see us joust."

"Go on, Daegel," said the man called Evan. "I'll join you in a minute."

"Nay," protested Daegel. "We are expected to go to the tiltyard together."

"Maggie, Maggie," called out Charles, pushing his way through the crowd to join her. "Oh, good, you found Emma."

"Who are you?" asked the knight.

Before Maggie could answer, Charles spoke up. "Sir Knight, I am Charles Whitlock and this is my sister, Maggie, and her daughter, Emma. Is there really going to be a feast today that anyone can attend?"

"Charles, be quiet," scolded Maggie, finally managing to get her daughter to calm down. "Lord Evan, we don't want to stand in your way."

"It's Sir Evan now," he said, removing his helm, exposing his thick brown hair that fell down the back of his neck, ending in a wave or slight curl. He had a smattering of whiskers on his face, as if he'd forgotten or hadn't had the time to shave today. Exhaustion showed on his face. He looked as tired as Maggie felt right now. Still, those bright green eyes continued to stare right through her.

"I'm sorry, Sir Evan." Maggie attempted a curtsy with the bundle on her back and still holding her daughter. It was awkward to attempt this in the crowd and her ankle twisted. "Oh!" she gasped as she started to fall. The knight reached out with one hand and grabbed her arm, keeping her from falling and from dropping Emma.

"You seem to be a traveler." He eyed up all the things that she and Charles carried. "Are you from Hythe? I don't believe I've ever seen you before ... Maggie," he added, causing her eyes to snap up to his when he used her name.

"We're looking for a new home," Charles blurted out. "My sister is a midwife."

"Really." Sir Evan reached out and picked up the basket at Maggie's feet. "You don't want to lose this. I suppose these are your supplies?"

"Yes. Or at least what I could carry since we're traveling on foot."

"From where do you come?" he asked curiously.

"We're coming from Aborfield, but our real home is in Ashenden." Charles freely spilled their personal business to the knight before Maggie could warn him not to divulge such information. Her eyes swept the crowd, hoping to hell that no guards from Ashenden had followed them here.

"Charles, please, stay silent," warned Maggie, not wanting anyone to know they were originally from Ashenden. After all, her mother died there. Maggie's reputation would be sullied if anyone realized she was related to the midwife who was blamed for the loss of a noblewoman and her baby. "We have been traveling for years and living in many places," Maggie told Evan. "Now if you'd kindly let me have my basket, we will be on our way."

"Nay, Maggie! I'm hungry," whined her brother. "We haven't eaten in days. I want to stay for the free feast."

"You haven't eaten in days?" asked Evan with a frown. "Is this really so?"

"My brother exaggerates," said Maggie, faking a laugh even though the information was true. Still, she didn't like feeling so pathetic in front of so many people. Especially not the nobles.

"Everyone is invited. By all means, you should stay for the feast," Evan told her, extending an arm to encompass the crowd.

"Thank you, but it'll be night soon and we need to find a place to stay before the sun sets." Maggie hated traveling in the dark. She also despised sleeping on the ground, exposed to any bandits or ruffians who inhabited the night. It was too dangerous, and she fought hard to protect her family in any way she could. They'd thankfully managed to secure sleeping arrangements in barns the last two nights. But the thought of bedding down in soiled hay and animal droppings yet again was just too much to bear. She needed to find somewhere better for her family to stay.

"Where is your husband, Maggie?" asked Evan, looking down at Emma.

"He's dead," she answered softly.

"Ah, a widow." Evan nodded and put a hand to his chin in thought.

"Yes," she answered. "I am a widow, Sir Knight."

"Are you the sole provider of both your daughter and your brother?" asked the knight.

"Yes," she answered softly, her mouth so dry she could barely swallow. "Since the death of our parents, I have been raising them on my own."

The knight's brows raised in surprise. "So you are orphans, too." He seemed deep in thought.

"Evan, the crowd awaits," said Daegel impatiently. "Leave this woman be. Let's get to the joust."

"Hold on," said Evan with a raised hand. "We just took our vows, promising to help both orphans and widows."

"Aye. So?" Daegel wrinkled his nose and shrugged.

"I knocked into the child and I could very well have hurt her."

"Nay. She's fine," Maggie answered, realizing everyone was staring at them now. She didn't like all this attention. It could only bring trouble upon them. "We'll be on our way now. Thank you, Sir Knight."

"Evan," he said, making her look back up at him.

"Pardon me?" she asked.

"Call me Sir Evan. Maggie." He'd used her name again, and for some reason it gave her a warm fluttering feeling in her belly. The man was a noble, a knight, and very handsome. Why was he paying her so much attention?

"Thank you. Sir Evan," she said, hoping to suffice the man so he'd leave her alone.

"Maggie, can we stay for the food? Please?" asked her brother. "I am so hungry that I could retch."

"Nay, Charles," she said from the side of her mouth. "Now let's go to town to see if we can find a place to camp for the night."

"Nay," said Evan in a form of finality. "You will be my guests and stay here at the castle tonight."

"What?" Maggie's eyes opened widely. Had she heard him wrong?

"Evan, you fool! What are you saying?" grumbled Daegel in a low voice.

"I have knightly duties now. I am going to help this widow," Evan insisted. "These poor orphans."

Maggie didn't like to be called a widow and hear Charles

and Emma called orphans aloud in front of so many people. She also didn't appreciate the condescending tone the man used, and the pity he held in his voice. It made her feel even worse than pathetic.

"There is no need for that, I assure you," she said, her anger and annoyance growing again. "I am a survivor, my lord. I have raised and supported my brother and daughter before, and I will continue to do so, even without your help." She turned to go, but stopped in her tracks when she heard his next words.

"The castle is in need of a midwife. I'd like to hire you, Maggie Whitlock."

"What?" she asked, feeling her heart about beating out of her chest from excitement. Was he really offering her food, a place to sleep, and now a job too? She slowly turned to face the man. This could be the answer to all her problems.

"Of course, if you take the job as castle midwife, you'd be required to live here at the castle," he continued.

"I would? What about my brother? And daughter?" she asked, looking at him from the side of her eyes. "I won't abandon them."

"And neither shall you have to," he answered with a smile. "They are welcome to stay here with you."

"Will meals be included?" asked Charles, basically drooling at the thought.

"Yes. Yes, they will," said Evan with a low chuckle.

"Cousin, what are you doing?" asked Daegel, giving Evan a disapproving gaze. "Your father won't like this. Besides, the castle already has a midwife."

"You do?" Maggie's heart sank. So, this really was too

good to be true. "Then I suppose you won't need me after all."

"Nay, that's not true," Evan told her. "My cousin, Lady Martine, is in residence at Saltwood Castle right now. You see, she is eight months pregnant and in need of proper care."

"Really?" This got Maggie's attention.

"Yes. She could use her own personal midwife. I'd like to hire you to be there for Lady Martine when she births her baby."

"Do it," Charles urged her. "Say yes, Maggie. You'll have a job and we'll have food again and a warm place to rest our heads."

"I'm hungry and tired, Mama," came Emma's little voice, as she looked up at Maggie with those sad, big brown eyes.

"Well, I don't know," said Maggie letting out a deep sigh. "Sir Knight, are you sure your father will agree to this?" After hearing Daegel's warning, she half-expected trouble. "After all, I hear that your father is the Lord Warden of the Cinque Ports. A very important man. Shouldn't you discuss these plans with him first?"

"Nay. Not at all." Evan laughed and waved a hand through the air. "Now, are you going to accept my offer or not?"

"I'm not sure. Would this just be a temporary position? Until Lady Martine births her baby?"

"I don't know. It could be. Or it could mayhap last forever. I mean, let's just see how it goes. Do you want the job?"

"You haven't even asked me my fee yet."

"It doesn't matter," said Evan. "No fee is too much when it comes to my cousin, Lady Martine."

"My, I'm sure Martine will love to hear you say that," sneered Daegel.

"I have a joust to get to, so please give me your answer anon." Evan stared at her with those bright green eyes, and every second felt like eternity to her. Her heart kept beating quickly and the sound of her blood rushing to her ears was so loud that she no longer even hear the voices of the gossiping crowd. Charles tugged at her sleeve, urging her to give the right answer. Still, Maggie wasn't sure this was really a good idea at all. She didn't even know if this knight really had the authority to hire her and give them meals and a place inside the castle to sleep. Once again, it sounded too good to be true and that made her more than a little leery.

"Mama," said Emma, raising her head from Maggie's chest. The little girl's arms wrapped around Maggie's neck. "That knight is nice. Can we stop walking all the time and just stay here with him?"

"Is that what you want, sweetheart?" She pushed a stray strand of blonde hair from her little girl's eyes.

"It's what I want," said Charles, looking upset that she hadn't asked him.

"Me too," said Emma, sadness showing on her face. "I saw other children here, so mayhap I can have a friend. And the dog I chased wanted to play with me."

"You wanted to play with a dog?" asked Maggie. "Is that why you strayed from Charles?" Her heart went out to her daughter. The poor little girl was so lonely and her brother was so hungry that it made her want to cry. Accepting the knight's offer, she'd have a job again and could stop looking.

They'd have a home and a place to sleep that was safe and secure. It wouldn't matter if the money was all gone, because living at the castle they'd have plenty of food and drink. She wouldn't have to worry about any of these things anymore. Even though a little voice in her head warned her not to do it, she looked up at the knight and nodded. "Thank you, Sir Evan. I think we will accept your offer."

CHAPTER 2

"Egads, Evan what is the matter with you?" Daegel spoke from atop his horse as he and Evan rode to the tiltyard to engage in the joust. "You can't be giving commoners you don't even know a home at Saltwood, not to mention a job. That just isn't done. You might be a knight now, but you have no authority to do that."

"I told you, we took vows today to help widows and orphans. I felt it was necessary."

"I'm sure the castle courtyard is filled with both widows and orphans right now. Are you going to make that offer to all of them?"

"Nay, of course not. But I knocked into the little girl and she fell in the mud. I feel bad about it."

"Just leave it be. The child most likely knocked into you."

"Nay. I don't think so." Evan looked out at the cheering crowd. He waved his hand in the air as they made their way to the lists, feeling grateful that so many seemed so happy to see him knighted. "I know it is odd, but for some reason I find the little girl's mother intriguing."

"There are more than enough pretty lightskirts at the castle if you need a good bedding," said Daegel. "Why on earth do you want to saddle yourself with one who has so much baggage? The little girl alone will prove to be quite an unwanted distraction, not to mention her unruly brother."

"Calm down, Daegel. I didn't say I was going to marry the wench, did I? I just want to show that I am loyal to my vows. And that I'm a good knight." They stopped their horses inside the tiltyard, and their squires ran over to greet them.

"Oooooh, so that's what it's all about. I see it clearly now," said Daegel with a slight chuckle. "You are trying to make the people think you are a far better knight than me, aren't you?"

"Nay. Of course not. It's not a competition."

"You say that, but somehow I don't think you really mean it. Besides, isn't the joust just that? A competition? Get in the spirit of it all, Evan." Daegel slipped his helm over his head. The long white plume atop the helm moved back and forth in the breeze. Then he retrieved his jousting lance and shield from his squire. "I'll stop any rumors about you being better before they even start."

"What does that mean?" asked Evan.

"As soon as I beat you at the joust, like we both know I will, everyone will see who is the better knight, after all."

"We are both knights now, and there is no reason to prove that either of us is better," ground out Evan, not wanting any problems today of all days.

Evan knew Daegel would probably best him in the joust,

since he truly was better at it. That was no secret. Still, he didn't really care. Or so he thought. His eye caught Maggie making her way to the front of the crowd, and suddenly his pride made him want to impress her. She slid onto one of the benches of the viewing stands, pulling her daughter atop her lap. Her brother munched on an apple and squeezed in next to her.

"Giles," Evan summoned his squire.

"Yes, my lord? I mean, Sir Evan?"

His new squire was a boy who looked not much older than Maggie's brother. He was tall and lanky with dark hair. Evan knew him as the son of one of his father's noble friends. The boy was fair with a weapon in his hand and lithe on his feet. Still, Evan had a lot to teach him, since he knew the boy often got much too anxious and lacked any amount of confidence. His being Evan's squire was a favor to a friend. Still, his squire needed to be skilled enough to protect Evan on the battlefield. Plus, he didn't want the boy to lose his life. He had a lot of training to do. Evan remembered his first days of being a squire and how nervous he was, hoping not to do anything wrong. He couldn't even imagine how Giles felt right now.

"Giles, if I start losing too bad to Sir Daegel at the joust, do me a favor. Stand in front of that woman holding the little girl and block her view." He nodded to Maggie.

"Pardon me, my lord?" Giles looked up with a puzzled expression and then followed Evan's gaze over to where Maggie sat watching. "You want me to do what?"

"Never mind," mumbled Evan, putting on his helm and slapping down the visor. Atop his helm were three plumes. One red, one gold, and the other blue. These were the colors of the Confederation of the Cinque Ports' coat of arms. Evan hoped to one day follow in his father's footsteps and become a baron of the Cinque Ports as well. He took his lance, couching it under his right arm and positioning the grapper, the small ring that was right behind the hand-guard, over the lance-rest. The lance-rest was a hook attached to Evan's breast plate. This secured the lance during the charge and helped to maximize the force of the impact. Next, he took his shield from Giles in his left hand, making certain the lance passed through the notch cut out atop the shield. His squire secured the shield to his arm. Evan looked back once more to Maggie, hoping she wouldn't think he was naught but a fool by the time this joust was finished. He wasn't sure why he felt this way. But after knocking into the little girl and making her mother angry, he wanted to show the girl's mother that he was honorable and deserving to be respected.

Maggie held Emma on her lap, placing her basket filled with her midwife instruments at her feet. The blanket tied around her carrying their belongings stayed in place, but felt bulky and in the way with so many people crowded around her. Her muscles ached from having to carry their things as well as her child most of the way on their journey here. Her gown was now muddied from her daughter, making Maggie feel like a dirty, homeless peasant around so many nobles and people dressed fancily for the day's occasion. Tiredness gripped her, consuming her so much that she no longer even felt the hunger pangs of not having eaten in a few days.

"Mama, I want an apple too, like Charlie has," whined the little girl, frowning at the boy.

"Charles," said Maggie, always calling her brother by his full name. She wasn't sure why she did it, but mayhap it was because it sounded like she spoke with more authority when she called him by his Christian-born name. After all, Maggie had taken the place of Charles's mother, and she almost felt as if he were more her son than her brother. Their age difference was seven years apart. "Where did you get that apple?"

"I didn't steal it, if that's what you mean." Charles took a big bite, making a loud crunching noise. Juice ran down his chin as he slurped it up and proceeded to lick his fingers.

"We don't have any food," Maggie pointed out. "So if you didn't swipe it, where did it come from? You don't have any money."

"Nay, but I didn't need it. I just smiled at a cute apple vendor girl and she gave it to me for free."

Emma started crying, probably from being overtired and famished.

"Share it with Emma, please," Maggie instructed, not even paying attention to the joust. "Once the feast starts, there should be more than enough food to fill your bellies."

"Fine," said the boy, giving the little girl the apple. "When does the feast start? I'm starving. I want to be the first one in line."

"I would imagine it will be right after the joust," said Maggie. "I saw some of the servants starting to set up trestle tables in the courtyard."

The crowd cheered loudly, gaining her attention. When she looked up at the jousting field, Sir Daegel was riding proudly with his lance held high in the air. However, it seemed to be broken. Sir Evan's lance wasn't broken or splintered at all. He, on the other hand, wasn't urging the crowd on. Matter of fact, he didn't ride as if he were happy, like Sir Daegel.

"Sir Daegel's lance looks broken," said Charles. "That's not good, is it?"

"I don't know. Probably not," said Maggie, not really caring. "I would imagine it is better to keep their lances intact."

The second pass came and Sir Evan's lance broke. Evan raised the pole in the air and got the crowd to cheer for him now. But then the herald announced that Sir Evan would not receive points, since the lance had broken crosswise and not from striking with the point. Some of the crowd cheered while others booed. Maggie remained confused about the rules of this silly and violent game.

On the third pass, Sir Daegel's lance splintered again. Sir Evan looked over at her, and even though his face was covered by his helm, Maggie got the impression from his body language that he wasn't happy.

"Sir Daegel looks happy that his lance splintered," said Charles, trying to understand the joust as well, and not being able to make much sense of it. "Mayhap it is a good thing after all."

"That's ridiculous. Why would breaking one's weapon be good?" asked Maggie. "This whole joust is just too violent. I don't want Emma watching it any longer. Let's go back to the courtyard and wait for the feast to begin." She stood up with Maggie in her arms. Charles, wanting food, was more than happy to follow.

• • •

Evan glanced over to see Maggie getting up to leave. Why did this bother him so much? Probably because he was losing the joust to his cousin. He wanted to look good in her eyes, but since she was leaving, it was obvious that she was already disappointed by his performance. Damn. All he needed on this last pass was to unseat Daegel, and he could still have a shot at winning. Determined to do so before she left the joust, he charged his horse down the field toward Daegel, leaning forward and giving it his all.

Once again, Evan felt the tip of Daegel's lance smash against his shield and heard the sickening sound of splintering wood. With all his might, he leaned into his thrust, managing to hit Daegel, but not break his own lance. However, his lance slid upward. Before Evan knew what happened, he saw Daegel almost falling off his horse as his helm fell from his head and hit the dirt.

Evan turned and looked back to see the herald raising his hands in the air and announcing the result of the joust as being a tie. This was because Evan had luckily managed to unhelm his competition.

"Yes!" Evan ripped off his helm, and immediately his gaze shot over to the stands as he searched for Maggie. He might not have won the joust, but being a tie was the next best thing. Now he wouldn't look like a loser in her eyes. He raised his hand in the air and acknowledged the crowd, making his way back to his squire.

"Good job, my lord," said Giles, rushing forward to take his helm.

"Squire, where is that woman I pointed out to you earlier? I don't see her anywhere." He continued to search the crowd but could not find her.

"Oh, the woman with the little girl on her lap who was sitting in the front row?"

"Yes, that is she," answered Evan.

"I believe she left, my lord." Giles took the lance from Evan and helped him to unbuckle the shield.

"She left? Really?" he asked. "When? Do you know if she saw the end of the joust?"

"I'm not really sure, my lord. However, I don't think so. She seemed uninterested in the joust. I saw her stand up before your final pass."

"Uninterested?" Evan's heart dropped. How could anyone be uninterested in the joust and actually leave before it was finished? Maggie Whitlock was only a commoner, but something about her was different from anyone he had ever met. She didn't seem to care much about things like praising nobles, being in the presence of knights, and doing whatever it took to be noticed in the eyes of titled men and women. This intrigued him even more, and also made him more than determined to get her to notice him and admire him like everyone else. The wench was very pretty, even with the mud on her gown and all the dust from the road. Her eyes were bright-blue and piercing, reminding him of a bird. Her hair was so light that it almost seemed to glow like a halo around the head of an angel. However, this woman certainly didn't act like an angel. She'd stood up to him, becoming as fierce as a lion when it came to protecting her daughter. Nay, Maggie Whitlock the widow was strong and the furthest thing from frail. The girl was also sassy, and somehow that seemed to him to be refreshing. He didn't want her walking out of his life so soon when she'd just wandered into it. "Find her, Giles. I need to talk with her."

"My lord?" His squire looked confused. "I need to tend to your horse and weapons and help you remove your armor so I can polish it."

"I'll manage for now," he said, dismounting. "Find the girl and her brother and the daughter. When you do, bring them directly to me in the great hall."

"Are you sure, my lord? I mean, I wasn't told hunting down wenches was to be part of my training."

"Are you questioning a knight?" he asked, not meaning to scare the boy, but training him to serve him without asking questions, since it was an important aspect of being a squire.

"Nay, my lord. I'm sorry. I'll go anon." Giles bowed and ran off to carry out his orders.

"Well, Cousin, you lucked out when my helm fell off," said Daegel, riding up to join him. "But don't think you'll be so lucky in the sword fight tomorrow."

"It wasn't luck, it was skill," scoffed Evan. "However, you'll need all the luck you can get when we fight with our blades ,since we both know I've got the upper hand with that." His eyes roamed over once again to where Maggie had been sitting. She really had left although he couldn't imagine why.

"You'll need luck too, Evan."

"Huh?" He turned back and made a face. "Nay, I won't. We both know I'm better with a blade than you are."

"I wasn't talking about sparring. I meant with the wench. I am talking about that widowed midwife who has seemed to besot you."

"Besot me? I am not besotted," he said. "I don't know what you're talking about."

"Don't bother lying to me, because I know differently. I saw the way you kept looking over at her during the joust. If you'd been paying more attention to me instead of her, you might have actually had a slight chance of winning. Slight."

"It is time for everyone to join us for the celebration feast," came Evan's father's voice, as he stood upon the dais, shouting so everyone could hear. "The knights and nobles and the occupants of Saltwood Castle will dine in the great hall. All others will eat in the courtyard. Enjoy."

"Did you tell your father yet that you've hired a midwife and are allowing the wench and her family to actually live at the castle?" asked Daegel with a smirk.

"Nay, not yet. But don't worry about it. I'll tell him," said Evan, unbuckling his arm-plate and looking over at his father, who was making a beeline straight for him with Daegel's father, Lord Corbett, at his side.

"Hmmm. Now, might be a good time for that," said Daegel with a chuckle. "Before we get to the great hall and he finds out for himself." Daegel stopped to talk to his father while Evan's father joined him.

"Good job, Son." Lord Garrett hit Evan on the back.

"It was a tie, Father. I didn't win."

"I know that. I'm talking about taking your vows today, not the results of the joust. I believe you'll be a good knight, Evan. Just the way you showed that poor widow a little courtesy tells me you understand what it is to be a knight, after all. Come, let's get to the great hall for the feast." Garrett looked around. "Where is your squire? Doesn't he know he's supposed to be tending to your horse and helping you out of your armor?"

"Giles is on an errand for me," said Evan, bending down

to unclip the armor plates from his legs. "I told him to meet me in the great hall."

"What kind of errand can be more important than helping a new knight out of his armor?" asked Garrett, not happy at all. "I will have him replaced at once."

"Nay, Father, don't do that. It was what I wanted. Giles is just following orders."

Garrett motioned to another squire who ran over to help. Once Evan was out of his armor and the squire had tended to his horse and equipment, they walked together to the great hall.

"So. Do you want to tell me what is going on?" asked Garrett, smiling and nodding to the other nobles as they walked past even though Evan knew his father was feeling bothered by Evan's decision regarding his squire.

"I hired a midwife," Evan blurted out before he lost his nerve.

"What are you talking about? We already have a midwife at the castle," said Garrett.

"I thought since Martine will be birthing her baby here at Saltwood and since David is back home running the tavern, Martine should have a companion. You know, for extra care." He spoke of his cousin Martine's husband, who was a commoner and once an innkeeper. Now, David ran the tavern in the courtyard of Blake Castle that was built with him and his family in mind.

"You make no sense, Evan. Your sister Eleanor is Martine's companion. That is why Martine is here. Besides, there are plenty of handmaids to tend to her needs. Your cousin doesn't need extra care."

"All right, I'll be honest with you. Maggie—the widowed

midwife whose daughter I knocked down—is in need of a job."

"I see. Well, I'm sure she can find a job in town," said his father as they walked. "Midwives are always in demand."

"She is homeless, Father. With a young daughter as well as an adolescent brother to support."

Garrett stopped in his tracks and crossed his arms over his chest. "Evan, it isn't your choice or your responsibility to make such decisions. It is mine. And I say Martine will be fine. We don't need another midwife."

"Couldn't Maggie just stay here for a while?" asked Evan, not willing to give up so easily. "I mean, I feel I owe it to her after knocking her daughter into the mud."

"You are a noble and she is a commoner, if I must remind you. Evan, you don't owe her a damned thing."

"Well, I did take the vow today to help widows and orphans, right?"

"Yes. And I appreciate that, truly I do. But there are too many orphans and widows to be favoring just a few."

"This is different. This one is skilled," Evan pointed out to his father. "She's a midwife. Surely midwives are much sought-after. You just said yourself that they are in great demand."

"The good ones, yes," agreed his father.

"Then she can stay?"

"Evan, what do you even know about this girl?"

Evan looked down and brushed dirt from his sleeve as they continued to walk. "Well, nothing really."

"If her help was truly needed by Martine, then mayhap I'd agree to your crazy idea. However, I don't see the need for it."

"Well, I do." Evan would not give up.

His father sighed. "Let her stay for the feast, and she and her family can sleep in the great hall tonight. Come morning, she'll have to go."

"Yes, Father," said Evan, disheartened. He didn't see how he could fix this dire situation.

Once Evan got to the great hall, he spotted Giles talking and laughing with Maggie. A tinge of jealousy swept through him. Somehow he wished it was he who was talking with the girl and making her smile. Maggie's brother Charles was flirting with every kitchen maid who walked past with a tray of food. His eyes were on the food and not the wenches. Little Emma was running around the great hall with two other children, seeming to have a great time as they chased one of the castle's hounds.

"Oh, there you are, Sir Evan." Giles took Maggie's hand and headed toward him. "I brought the midwife here as you instructed." Their hand-holding seemed to linger and Evan didn't miss it.

"Thank you, Giles. Now get out of here. Go help the other squire tend to my armor and horse."

"Other squire?" Giles released Maggie's hand and his smile faded. "What other squire?"

"Don't worry, your position is not in peril. Or at least not yet, it's not," Evan told him. "However, if you stall any longer I might be finding myself with a new squire."

Giles's face reddened as he became flustered. "Nay, my lord. I mean, yes, my lord, I'll go at once," said Giles, running off to do his work and keep his job.

"Thank you, Sir Evan, for giving me a job and also a home for my family." Maggie seemed tired, but her words were sincere as she smiled widely at him. Her teeth were straight and white and beautiful. Her smile was like no other. "I want you to know that my brother Charles already likes it here. So does Emma. My daughter has always wanted friends, and already she seems to have made some." Her gaze roamed over to the little girl across the room.

"Yes," said Evan clearing his throat, the sight of the happy little bedraggled girl about melting his heart. "About that …"

Maggie turned to look at her daughter. "Emma, no, don't pull the dog's tail!" Maggie called out. "Excuse me, Sir Evan, but I need to stop my daughter before she gets bit." She hurried away, leaving Evan standing there by himself.

"Well, Brother, you and Daegel are finally knights. So tell me, how does it feel?" His sister, Eleanor, walked up to greet him, with their very pregnant cousin, Martine, at her side. Eleanor was a vision of beauty, her flaming red hair catching the eye of every man she'd ever passed by. Martine had dark hair and dainty features. Except for her overly large midsection right now. Still, she was a true beauty.

"It feels fine," said Evan, noticing that Martine was rubbing her belly and there was a grimace on her face. "Are you ill, Martine?"

"She's pregnant, not sick," snapped Eleanor, with a roll of her eyes. "If you ever get a wife of your own mayhap you'll start to understand the ways of women."

"I doubt it," he mumbled under his breath, never understanding why women always became so irritating at certain times of the month. His sister seemed to be the worst.

"Actually, Eleanor, I didn't want to say anything, but I

have been feeling ill lately," answered Martine, continuing to rub her belly.

"Do you think the baby is coming?" asked Evan.

"Nay, silly," said Eleanor. "Martine is not due for another month yet. It is much too early. I often felt ill when I was pregnant, too. I am sure it is only natural."

"Mayhap she should be looked at," said Evan. "I can call a midwife."

"I met with the midwife this morning," said Martine. "She said it was just discomfort from carrying the baby's weight, but I'm not sure. Oh, I wish David were here right now."

"Your husband will be here closer to the time of your birthing," Eleanor reminded her. "He is busy at the tavern. He'll be here soon, don't worry."

"To me, it feels like it'll be years," Martine answered, sounding extremely sad.

"I'm sorry I wasn't fast enough to keep my daughter from pulling the hound's tail," said Maggie, holding Emma in her arms as she approached. She couldn't see well past the child and obviously didn't realize Evan was talking to other nobles. The proper thing to do would be to wait off to the side until she was acknowledged by a noble before she even thought to speak.

Evan cleared his throat, causing her to peer around her daughter. "Oh, excuse me, I didn't mean to interrupt your conversation." She put her daughter down and curtsied.

"Maggie, this is my sister, Lady Eleanor and my cousin, Lady Martine," Evan introduced them. "Girls, this is Maggie Whitlock and her daughter, Emma, whom I almost ran over earlier."

"Hello," said Eleanor with a nod. "Are you here with the villagers for the celebration today?"

"Well, yes and no," she answered, sounding cautious. "I mean, this is my new home now, thanks to Sir Evan."

"What?" both the girls said together, staring at Evan.

"Maggie is a midwife," explained Evan.

"Yes, that's right," said Maggie, continuing to speak, not waiting to be spoken to. "Sir Evan hired me to take care of his pregnant cousin," said Maggie, her gaze dropping to Martine's waist as the woman continued to rub her belly. "Oh, I'm sorry, I believe that is you, Lady Martine. Am I right?"

"Yes, that's right," answered Martine.

Maggie walked closer. "You are carrying so low. You'll be giving birth very soon, no doubt."

"Soon?" Martine looked horrified.

"Nay, you're wrong. She isn't due for another month yet," interjected Eleanor.

"Another month?" Maggie's eyes remained on the pregnant woman's belly and her brow furrowed. "Who told you that?" Maggie's eyes flashed up to Martine's face and then down to her midsection again.

"It's what the midwife told me," Martine answered. "However, I have been feeling odd lately. The midwife said it is natural but I am afraid that something might be wrong," Martine's voice held great concern.

"Odd? How so?" Maggie wasn't afraid to ask questions.

"I feel ... heavier ... down there," she said in a whisper, seeming embarrassed to be speaking about this in front of Evan.

"Has the baby been moving a lot?" Maggie stepped right in, ignoring everyone but Martine.

"Oh, yes. Too much, actually," Martine told her. "The babe never seems to sleep."

"I see." Maggie put her hand to her chin. "Have you been feverish at all?"

"Feverish? I—I don't know," said Martine. "I don't think so."

"May I touch your forehead to check for fever?" Maggie asked permission. "I need to rule out internal infection."

"That is not a proper thing to do," scolded Eleanor.

"Nay, it's fine," said Martine in a shaky voice. "Yes, please do, Maggie. Check me for fever. I need to know that my baby's life isn't in peril." Martine held her chin up and brought her head closer to Maggie.

Maggie gently laid her hand on Martine's forehead and smiled as she quickly removed it. "I am happy to say there is no fever." Her gaze shot over to Evan. "Sir Evan, I would like to examine Lady Martine closer, because I believe her baby is coming much sooner than she believes. I have an idea why this might be so, but don't want to say anything until I am sure."

"Who are you to say our castle midwife is wrong?" Eleanor became haughty, and Evan didn't like that.

"She is just trying to help," he told his sister. "Perhaps a second opinion is worth considering."

"What are your credentials?" asked Eleanor, becoming suspicious. "We don't know anything about you except for your name. With whom did you train and where did you work? Why don't you have a job now? Who is your mother?"

Eleanor fired one question after another at Maggie without even giving her a chance to respond.

"Eleanor, stop it," warned Evan. "You are treating her like some sort of criminal, and I don't appreciate it."

"Nay, she has a right to know. You all do," said Maggie, suddenly seeming sad or mayhap nervous. "I trained with my mother, Margaret Whitlock, before her death. She was a respected midwife who was known for never losing a baby or a baby's mother. It was in … in Ashenden." Maggie quickly looked up at the nobles as if she were expecting some sort of reaction.

She played with a crystal pendant hanging from a cord around her neck as she spoke. Evan realized that the girl was acting odd all of a sudden, and had seemed to lose her confidence.

"I've never heard of your mother," stated Eleanor. "Have either of you?" she asked the other nobles.

"Nay," said Evan with a shrug. "Then again, I don't really know any midwives, since it never takes my concern."

"I haven't heard of her either, I'm sorry," answered Martine.

Maggie's jaw dropped open. She had been sure these nobles would have heard of her mother and what happened four years ago in Ashenden. After all, didn't nobles all know each other and talk things over? She had thought so. Maggie highly expected them to know that her mother was executed for losing a noblewoman and her baby because she'd neglected them to help Maggie's baby be born.

They hadn't. None of the three had any idea, and it was a

stroke of good luck for her. She wanted to be honest with them and so she'd told them the truth. Or part of it, anyway. Right now she didn't think she wanted to point out the doomed fate of her midwife mother and how she'd died.

"Well, I suppose we'll have to ask around and find out more about you, won't we?" asked Eleanor, making Maggie's heart drop once again.

Maggie's fingers clutched the crystal even harder. "Of course," said Maggie with a curtsy.

"Ooooh. I really don't feel well. I am having spasms." Martine held on to Eleanor and put her other hand on her belly.

"You need to lie down and rest," said Maggie. "I have an herbal ointment that will help ease the spasms. However, you need to get off your feet. It is crucial. Right now, until I can determine the cause of your discomfort, it is important that you stay in bed."

"Do you really think so?" asked Martine.

"Yes. Yes, I do," said Maggie. "And it is crucial that I examine you. It is for your own safety and for that of your baby."

"We will call for the castle midwife," Eleanor told Martine.

"Nay, you can't. She's gone and won't be back for a few days," explained Martine. "She had a family member giving birth in a neighboring village and I told her to go. After all, family is important."

Maggie liked to hear this coming from a noble. Most nobles thought their lives were the only ones important, and that commoners' lives and families didn't matter.

"Sir Evan, if you'd be kind enough to tell me where I'll be

staying, I'll put my bags in my room and quickly get cleaned up. Then I will examine Lady Martine."

"Oh, I'd appreciate that," said Martine, her breathing labored. "I only want the best for my baby. We need to be sure. I cannot wait for the castle midwife to return."

"I ... don't know," said Evan.

"What don't you know?" asked Evan's mother, Echo, walking over with a smile on her face as she joined them. She leaned over and kissed Evan on the cheek. "Congratulations, Son, on being knighted."

"Thank you, Mother," said Evan, returning the kiss and giving his mother a quick hug. Maggie liked the way he treated his mother. That said a lot about a man. "Mother, this is Maggie. She's a midwife," said Evan with a nod. "She's offered to help Martine who isn't feeling well."

"Hello, Maggie. Welcome," said Echo. "Martine? What's the matter?" Echo asked in surprise.

"I'm not sure, Lady Echo," answered Martine. "The castle midwife says I am not due for another month yet, but Maggie said my baby is coming much sooner."

"Do you really think so?" Echo asked Maggie.

"Yes, I do," said Maggie. "I have been attending births since I was six, and have finished my training as a midwife at sixteen."

"That's amazing," said Echo. "Then mayhap you should take a look at Lady Martine."

"Yes, I'd like to examine Lady Martine to insure her baby is fine," agreed Maggie.

"Evan has already hired the midwife and offered her a room in the castle, yet he knows nothing about her," Eleanor relayed the information to her mother.

"Martine, do you want Maggie's help?" asked Echo.

"I do," answered Martine. "I would feel better knowing someone as skilled as she is by my side."

"Then we will make it so." Echo raised her hand and summoned the castle steward. "Stefan, please take Maggie and her things to one of the empty servant's rooms off the kitchen."

"Aye, my lady," said Stefan with a bow.

"Thank you, my lady," said Maggie in relief, taking the hand of her daughter. "I'll just call to my brother to bring the rest of our things."

"Oh, you have family here," said Echo. "I didn't realize that."

"I hope it isn't a problem." Maggie hoped the woman wouldn't change her mind, knowing there would be three of them to house and feed instead of just one.

"Nay, of course not, my dear." Lady Echo was a true joy to be around. "We welcome you and your family to Salt-wood Castle and hope you will enjoy your time here."

Maggie found herself still clutching her crystal, believing that this truly was a lucky charm after all. She went from being homeless, hungry, and jobless one minute, to having the best offer ever the next. Now, she just hoped no one would ever discover who her mother had truly been or it might ruin Maggie's reputation. If so, all her luck could change quickly, and this time not for the better.

CHAPTER 3

"What do you think?" Martine asked Maggie an hour later from her bed. "Will my baby be all right?" She pushed up to her elbows. Eleanor and a hand-maid were in the room as well.

"Just a moment," said Maggie, gently placing her hands on various parts of Martine's belly to feel the movement of the baby. Maggie wore a long white apron over her gown. It was what she used when delivering babies. Her hair was pinned up and she wore a white head wrap over her hair that was a cross between a wimple and a hood. "Mmm hmm. Interesting," she spoke to herself.

"What's interesting?" asked Martine. "Please tell me that everything is all right."

"It is more than all right." Maggie put Martine's gown back into place. "Actually, I think it is very exciting." Maggie got up and walked over to clean her hands in a basin of water. Then she picked up a towel to dry them.

"Well, are you going to tell us or make us guess?" asked Eleanor from the other side of the room.

"Please, tell me," begged Martine. "Even if it is not good news. I need to know."

Maggie smiled widely. "I was right," she said. "You are going to give birth any day now."

"So you're saying the castle midwife was wrong about my cousin's delivery date?" Eleanor walked over to the bed.

"Nay, not really. She was right. Mainly."

"Oh, Maggie, I don't understand and cannot take the suspense anymore." Martine grabbed Maggie's arm and pulled her closer. "Please, tell me everything."

"All right," said Maggie, sitting down on the edge of the bed. "You really are only eight months pregnant, that part is true. However, you will be giving birth most likely within the next week."

"That makes no sense," snapped Eleanor. "If that is so, then something must be wrong. No baby is born that early."

"If we're talking about just one baby, you're right," explained Maggie, taking Martine's hand in hers. "But Lady Martine is not having just one baby. She is going to be birthing two."

"Twins?" Martine shot up to a sitting position, then grabbed her belly and moaned.

"You need to lie back down and rest," said Maggie, helping Martine get settled with her back against the pillows.

"I am going to have two babies? Really?" she gushed.

"Yes. I've seen this before and I am sure of it," Maggie answered. "That is why you feel so heavy. The weight of two babies, plus the fact they are running out of room to grow, will cause them to be born early."

"Is that dangerous?" asked Eleanor, taking Martine's other hand in hers.

"I am not going to lie. Birth is always dangerous. No matter if it is one, two, or three babies at a time," Maggie told them in a serious voice. "However, from my exam I am fairly certain that both of your babies, Lady Martine, are alive and healthy."

"I'm going to have twins," said Martine, lying back down, looking as if she were in shock. "Just like my brother Robin's wife, Sage. But her twins will be born after mine. This is unbelievable."

"I'll say. Two sets of twins in the same family?" asked Maggie, surprised at hearing this news.

"Lady Martine's father, Lord Madoc, is a twin to my mother, Lady Echo," Eleanor relayed the information.

"Well, then that explains it." Maggie released Martine's hand and stood up. "Good luck with the babies. I wish you the best."

"I have to send a pigeon right away to tell David," mumbled Martine from the bed, speaking about her husband.

"A pigeon?" Maggie smiled, since it sounded so odd.

"Our entire family communicates from one part of the land to the other by sending messages with carrier pigeons from castle to castle," Eleanor explained.

"Yes. My father used to raise and race pigeons all his life," Martine told her. "It was his idea to construct a dovecote at each of our family's castles."

"What a great idea!" Maggie went over to her bag and opened it, digging inside. There was a knock at the door.

"See who it is," Eleanor told the handmaid.

When the handmaid opened the door, Maggie heard a man's voice from out in the corridor.

"Let me in," said Evan, pushing his way into the chamber with Daegel following on his heels.

"Brother! You shouldn't be in here," scolded Eleanor.

"I don't care," grumbled Evan. "You've all been in here so long that the meal is nearly over. Is everything all right?"

"Yes, tell us. What is going on?" asked Daegel. "Aunt Echo is really worried about Martine."

"Everything is fine," Maggie assured them, finding what she was looking for and pulling it out of her bag. "Martine, however is confined to bed rest until she gives birth. It is for her own safety, as well as for the benefit of the babies."

"Babies? Did you say babies?" asked Evan. "As in more than one?" He raised a craggy brow.

Martine smiled from her prone position on the bed. "Yes, Cousin. I am having twins, just like my brother, Robin, and Sage. Isn't that wonderful?"

"Yes. Wonderful," said Evan, saying the words but not showing the emotion on his face.

"I thought twins were considered a bad thing." Daegel plopped down in a chair and rested one leg over the arm of the chair. "I always heard that giving birth to more than one baby at a time meant the children were spawned by the devil."

"What?" Martine looked as if she were going to cry.

• • •

Evan elbowed Daegel in the ribs and glowered at him. "Shut up, you fool," he said from the side of his mouth. Then walking over to the bed he tried to calm down his cousin. "Daegel doesn't know what he's saying. Twins just means you'll be blessed twice. Right, Maggie?" He looked over to her, hoping to hell she'd support him. The last thing they needed was a terrified, panicky, pregnant woman on their hands.

"Of course it does." Maggie unwound what looked like a long belt made out of silk. It seemed to have words and sentences written all over it.

"What in the name of the devil is that?" asked Evan, thinking it was the silliest thing he'd ever seen.

"Don't say *devil*," she mumbled, glaring at him from the side of her eyes and pointing out that wasn't the best thing to say right now. "It is a birthing girdle." Maggie brought it over to the bed and started wrapping it around Martine's waist.

"A what?" asked Daegel, making a face like he'd smelled the garderobes on a hot summer day.

"It looks like someone wrote all over that belt," remarked Evan.

"That's true," answered Maggie. "It is inscribed with prayers and invocations." She looked back over her shoulder as she helped Martine secure it around her waist, tying a knot in front.

"I don't understand this at all," admitted Evan.

"It's for protection," continued Maggie. "To ensure safe delivery for the babies. There you are." She finished tying it and stood up.

"That sure sounds like the works of the devil to me,"

mumbled Daegel, once again getting a look that could kill from both Evan and Maggie this time.

"So, it's for good luck?" asked Eleanor.

"Exactly," Maggie answered with a smile.

"Did you wear one of those birthing girdles when you gave birth to your daughter?" Evan asked her curiously.

"Nay." Maggie's smile quickly turned into a frown. Her hand went to her chest and she caressed the crystal pendant hanging from the cord around her neck. "I had another good luck charm instead."

"Is that a crystal pendant?" Evan walked over and picked up the crystal in his hand to inspect it. The long shard was pointed at the tip and was so clear that he could see right through it.

"It is," said Maggie. "My mother gave it to me when I was pregnant with Emma.

"And you somehow believe this crystal brought you good luck? Really?" Evan didn't believe in charms and such nonsense.

"Yes, I do believe it," she told him.

"It is just a bunch of silly superstition." Evan often scoffed at people who were superstitious and did addled things to supposedly protect themselves. He believed a person brought on their own luck by their thoughts.

"The crystal pendant used to be my mother's," Maggie spoke softly. She sounded so sad that it took Evan's attention. He looked down at her, staring into her bright blue eyes. There he witnessed deep grief and what he believed to be pain that she tried to hide. He wanted to ask her about it, but decided to do it later in private. Somehow he didn't think she'd tell him much with the others listening. Maggie seemed to be a private kind of girl.

"You look tired," he told her, releasing her crystal pendant and letting it settle again against her chest.

"It's been a long day," she admitted, directing her gaze in the opposite direction instead of looking directly at him.

"You must be hungry," he said. "All of you." He looked over to the other women in the room. "I've already instructed a kitchen maid to bring food to you here in the bedchamber since you missed the meal."

"Good," said Maggie. "That will be perfect for Martine, since she really needs to stay in bed. If she doesn't, she'll risk having the twins even earlier, which might not be good." Maggie packed up her things, and picked up her bag as well as her midwife basket that was filled with her tools and ointments. "Lady Martine, I am leaving this herbal cream here for your handmaid to apply to your belly twice a day." She put the jar on the bedside table. "It will aid in making your skin more flexible to help with the stretch marks and to keep you from scarring."

"Thank you, Maggie," said Martine, with tears of joy in her eyes. "You have made me very happy. It is a blessing that you showed up in my life. I feel much better now, knowing why I was feeling so odd. I am so excited to be carrying twins. Maggie, I want you here by my side until after I give birth. That would put my mind at ease."

"I will only stay until the castle midwife returns," Maggie told her, looking down at her bag rather than to look at Martine. "I never intended to steal anyone's job."

"You're planning on leaving?" asked Evan in surprise, this being the last thing he expected to hear.

"Yes," she told him. "We both know that this is only a temporary job. I need a permanent one in order to support my daughter and brother." Maggie sighed. "I will go to town first thing in the morning to see if my services are needed there."

"Oh, Maggie, I want you for my midwife," cried Martine as Maggie headed for the door.

"I will fill in for now, but it is not an ideal situation for me to stay when the castle already has a midwife. I wouldn't like someone pushing me out of a job. I am sorry but I won't do it to anyone else."

"We understand," said Eleanor.

Maggie opened the door to find a kitchen maid standing there with a tray of food. The servant looked into the room but did not enter. "Sir Evan, I've brought the food and drink as instructed," said the girl.

"Thank you. Bring it over to the bed for the ladies." Evan walked to the door and took Maggie's arm as the kitchen wench entered with the tray of food. "Maggie, wait. Are you sure you won't stay for something to eat? I know you must be starving."

"It wouldn't be appropriate for me to eat with nobles," she told him. "Besides, Charles has been watching Emma for me and he tends to let her wander off. It is time I put her to bed."

"Then at least let me escort you to your room." Evan stepped out into the corridor and closed the door behind him. They walked in silence down the hall, taking the back stairway that led to the servants' quarters off the kitchen. "You were wonderful in there, Maggie. Martine already looks and is acting so much better. It is all because of you."

"I was just doing my job," she said over her shoulder, leading the way down the stairs. They entered the kitchen and when the servants saw Evan, they all stopped what they were doing to bow or curtsy as he passed through.

"Mama!" cried Emma, climbing down from atop a stool and running over to hug Maggie. There was flour all over her hands and face.

"What have you been doing?" Maggie scolded, picking up her daughter and brushing her off. "And why isn't Charles watching you like he's supposed to be doing?"

"Charlie is eating pie with the pretty lady," said the little girl, pointing a dirty finger across the room. Sure enough, Charles had his back to them, not even watching Emma. He was by the hearth, flirting with one of the kitchen maids. In his hands were the remnants of what looked like an apple pie. He clutched a spoon and shoveled the food into his mouth, his gaze fastened on the pretty servant the entire time.

Maggie let out a deep sigh. "God help me," she said under her breath. "Charles, come here!"

Charles spun around so fast that he almost dropped the plate from the pie. He shoved it into the kitchen maid's hands and wiped his mouth with his sleeve.

"Maggie," he said, running over to her. "You've got to taste the pie. It is better than any I have ever had."

"You were supposed to be watching Emma," she reprimanded him. "She could have wandered off or disappeared."

"I *was* watching her." Charles looked over at the little girl and started laughing. "Oh, it seems she was trying to make a pie of her own."

"Take her to our room and clean her up and get her to bed," Maggie instructed, pushing Emma into the boy's arms.

"Fine," said Charles with a sigh. "Are you coming too, Maggie?"

"I'll be there as soon as I have a word with Sir Evan."

"All right," said the boy, leaving for their room with Emma in his arms.

"Sir Evan, I'd like to take a trip into town tomorrow to look for a job, and I was wondering if you knew of any vendors that might be going that way. Mayhap they'd be kind enough to give me a ride."

"I'll take you," he offered. "I have to go to town to collect the rents anyway. We'll leave right after the swordfight that is scheduled in the morning between me and Sir Daegel."

"Swordfight?" Her head snapped up. That undeniable look of disapproval washed over her face again.

"Yes. It's just sparring, really," he told her. "It's expected as a form of entertainment for the other soldiers, nothing else."

"You seem to engage in a lot of dangerous forms of entertainment." She yawned.

"I am a knight, Maggie. Danger is part of my life."

"Well, I don't like my daughter seeing so much violence. That is another reason why I don't think we'll be staying at the castle. But thank you for your offer."

"I see." Evan didn't know what to say to that. He'd never heard of anyone in their right mind giving up a job, free meals, and a home at a castle just because they thought things were too violent there.

"If you'll excuse me, I need to check on my daughter."

"Wait," said Evan, grabbing a platter of fruit, bread, and sweetmeats from a passing serving wench and handing it to Maggie. "You need to eat as well."

Maggie looked down to the food in her hands and nodded. "Thank you, and good night," she said with another yawn, turning to leave.

"Thank you for everything today," he called after her, not wanting her to leave.

"What?" she asked, turning back once more.

"I mean, thanks for helping Lady Martine and all."

"I told you, it is my job."

"You need something to drink as well." Evan looked back and saw a bottle of wine on the table. He snatched it up and handed it to Maggie. He was quickly running out of ideas to get her to stay. "It'll help you relax so you can get some sleep."

"Her hands were filled with the food, wine, and her basket. "Believe me, I'll have no trouble sleeping tonight. I imagine I'll be asleep before my head hits the pillow. Good night, then." She turned her back to him and headed to her room.

Maggie stopped outside the door to her tiny room and looked back across the kitchen. Evan left, heading back out to the great hall to be with the other nobles. With him went that feeling of excitement inside her whenever he was near. Her heart swelled, looking at the food and wine he'd made sure she had since she'd missed the meal. Evan seemed to care about her, even though he didn't even know her. When he'd touched her crystal earlier, it almost seemed like an intimate act to her. He'd been standing so close to her that she could actually feel his body heat encompass her. He'd smelled like woodsmoke and leather, mixed with pine and fresh air from the outdoors. Never had those scents affected her in such a positive manner like they did today.

She shouldn't like being around him, but she did. Maggie usually despised nobles, ever since what happened to her mother. But something about Evan made her question her choices. Something almost seemed to be changing within her since she realized she liked this man called Sir Evan. Part of her wanted more than anything to take up his offer to stay here at the castle. However, if she did that, she felt it would be a mistake. It would be like betraying her departed mother to side with nobles. True, these nobles weren't the same as the ones she'd left behind, but it didn't matter. They were all the same. Arrogant, rude, haughty, and quick to blame a commoner for all their woes. Aiding Lady Martine until the castle midwife returned would be as far as this would go, she decided. To stay here forever was something that would only bring her sorrow, and she knew it.

Sooner or later someone here at Saltwood Castle would most likely figure out what had happened with her mother. Nobles talked and gossiped mayhap even more than nosey alewives. Honestly, she was surprised that word from Ashenden hadn't already reached here by now. After all, it had been four years! When these nobles finally did find out, Maggie's reputation would be ruined for sure. If so, she might never get a job again, no matter what town she stopped in. That's why she was better off always being on the move. The devil was on her heels, and she wouldn't let him ever catch her and her family.

A new job in town or the village wouldn't make her much money, but it was safer for now for her to be a midwife to the merchants or tradespeople instead of for the nobles. If commoners knew the truth, they wouldn't care.

Nobles were always blaming their misfortunes on those below the salt. She'd seen that the day her daughter was born. The day her mother lost everything because of a noble's misfortune. Maggie had left Ashenden that day with her brother and daughter, just like her mother had told her to do, and she'd never returned. She'd heard the bells ringing the warning when the noblewoman and her baby died. It was to let everyone know there would be an execution. That is, the killing of a poor midwife who had done nothing wrong. She was sure the nobles had no regrets taking her mother's life, even though her mother was the same midwife who had brought so many babies safely into this world without a problem. Her mother had helped so many mothers heal and go on to live and take care of those same children.

Life was hard, cruel, and unfair, and Maggie didn't expect it ever to get any better. She would be on the run until the day she died, but she had to do it. Her only concern was not for herself, but only for Charles and Emma. She was their provider. Their protector. They counted on her to survive. The last thing Maggie ever wanted was to be taken away from Charles and Emma the way her mother had been ripped away from them.

Nay, Maggie decided, she wouldn't stay at Saltwood Castle, even if it was very tempting to do so. Because she knew anything that seemed too good to be true usually was, and this time would be no different. She'd pushed down her attraction to Sir Evan, even though the man had done nothing wrong. But to stay here, to accept Sir Evan's offer, would feel like she'd be hurting her fond memories of her dear mother. Nobles were no good, and she wanted nothing to do with them. Maggie swore she would never trust another one as long as she lived. Nay, not even the handsome knight, Sir Evan Blackmore of Saltwood Castle.

CHAPTER 4

Evan's mind wasn't on the sword fight this morning, but rather stuck on the fact that Maggie didn't like him enough to want to take him up on his offer. What did he do that was so bad that he was scaring her away? He thought he'd made up for knocking down her little girl, even though he couldn't quite remember if he'd told her he was sorry. Then again, as a noble, he wasn't expected to apologize to a commoner.

"Sir Evan? Sir Evan?" called out his squire, waving his hand in front of Evan's face. They stood in the same field where the joust had taken place yesterday. The swordplay would be fast and easy today, and Evan wasn't worried about it at all.

"Giles, what is it? And do you really need to wave your hand in front of my face?" he ground out.

"Sorry, my lord." The boy lowered his hand. "It's just that Sir Daegel is waiting in the field and the crowd is becoming impatient for the show."

"All right, let's get this over with then." He took his sword from his squire, warming up his wrist by waving the sword around in a figure eight.

"Did you want me to block the view of you again?" asked Giles.

"What in the devil's name are talking about?" He turned and started to walk to the center of the field. Giles ran after him.

"I mean, did you want that wench to see you today or not?"

"What wench?" This squire always seemed to be talking, and Evan wasn't a small talk type of man. He'd never been so chatty when he was a squire. Squires should be seen but not heard. He had half a mind to tell Giles that too.

"The wench with the little girl. You know ... that pretty new midwife."

"Midwife?" That got his attention. He stopped in his tracks and spun around to face his squire. "Where? Where is she?"

"She's right there in the front row again." The squire pointed and Evan's attention followed. Sure enough, Maggie was sitting on the front bench wrapped in a cloak with her hood up over her head. She had her midwife basket of supplies on her lap today instead of her daughter. Charles didn't seem to be with her either. He figured she'd left little Emma behind with Charles, since she'd commented that swordplay and jousting was much too violent for her daughter to watch.

"I need to talk to her." He started in Maggie's direction.

"What about Sir Daegel?" Giles called out after him.

"I'll leave you to talk to Daegel. I have nothing to say to him."

Maggie saw Evan making a beeline toward her, and it caused her heart to jump in her chest. Quickly, she pulled her hood closer to cover her face, but it was too late. He'd already seen her. She had meant to stay hidden, but Evan seemed to always know exactly everything that was happening.

"Maggie, good morning," he said, with a smile that could brighten up anyone's day. "I didn't expect to see you here."

"Really? Why not?" she asked, too shaken to even return his greeting. She smoothed her skirts, aware of all the onlookers watching and listening. Damn, she didn't want all this attention.

"Oh, I don't know," he said, resting one arm on the wooden slated fence that was the barrier between the onlookers and those inside the part partitioned off for the knights and soldiers. "I figured you'd think this was too violent to watch."

He was using her words against her and she didn't like it.

"It *is* too violent, and that is why I did not bring my daughter or my brother with me," she said with a stiff upper lip.

"I see." He perused her and bit at his bottom lip. "Then you're really not that squeamish after all?"

"Squeamish? Of course, not. I am a midwife and have probably seen more blood than you have on a battlefield."

"Oh, really." He chuckled as if her words amused him, and she felt her anger rising.

"Sir Knight, I only wait here now because you are my ride to town as soon as this silly game of yours is over."

"Silly game?" He slowly lowered his arm from the fence. "I'll have you know that sparring with swords is not a game and neither is it silly." He raised his sword in the air, causing her to jerk backward in surprise. "This blade is sharp." He ran the back of his hand against the broad side of the sword. "This is a weapon. It can kill. The two edges of my sword also symbolize that a knight serves both God and his people."

He was causing a stir amongst the crowd and Maggie didn't like what he was doing.

"Well, I doubt that God would approve, but your people are waiting, so mayhap you should give them what they want," she told him.

"Evan! What on earth are you doing? Let's go," shouted Daegel, stretching his neck to see across the tiltyard. "You can flirt with the wenches later."

"Pipe down," Evan called out over his shoulder, then turned back to Maggie. "I am looking forward to our little outing today," he told her, making her feel even more uncomfortable since the crowd of people were moving closer to her on the bench, hoping to overhear something to include in their daily gossip.

"It is not an outing, Sir Evan. It is business only. If I must remind you, I am looking for a job."

"Evan!" Daegel called out again, waving his hands above his head this time, trying to get Evan's attention.

"I've got to go," Evan told her. "Just enjoy the show. I'm

going to grind Sir Daegel into the ground." He chuckled. "He can't beat me in a swordfight and he knows it. Now I'm going to prove it." He ran off, holding his sword in the air and nodding to the crowd. The spectators stood up and cheered, waving banners above their heads.

"I don't care to see anyone grind another into the dirt," mumbled Maggie, getting up with her basket and leaving behind the arrogant man and his dangerous show.

Evan fought like a lion, wanting to impress Maggie since he knew she was there watching. Plus, he needed to put his cousin in his place, since the joust yesterday was a little demeaning for him, even if it did end in a tie. He won the swordplay like he knew he would, sliding his blade into the sheath at his waist and waving both hands over his head, making the crowd cheer even louder. "Good job, Daegel, but you still can't beat me with a blade." Evan clamped arms with Daegel and slapped him on the back in a gesture of good will.

Daegel was sulking. "I'd like to beat you with something all right, and I promise you I am not speaking about a game."

Feeling good about himself, Evan turned to look over at Maggie, hoping he had impressed her. To his dismay, the seat where she'd been sitting was now empty.

"Did you want me to shine your sword, my lord?" Giles ran over, eager to do his job.

"Squire, where did that woman go?" he asked, still scanning the crowd for Maggie.

"The midwife?" asked Giles.

"Yes."

"Oh, she left even before you started to spar."

"She did?" Evan suddenly felt worse than before. "Why?"

"I don't know, my lord," the boy answered.

"Mayhap your ugly face scared her off," said Daegel, shining his sword with a rag. "After all, you don't have a lot of luck with the wenches, Evan. Especially the pretty ones."

"Bite your tongue, Daegel. I'm not talking to you." Evan turned to his squire. "Run ahead to the stable and saddle my horse."

"My lord? Are we going somewhere?" asked his squire.

"Yes. I will be collecting taxes from the proprietors in town today. Maggie will be joining us."

Daegel stopped polishing his sword and looked up curiously. "You're still not giving up on the wench, are you? Just face it, she doesn't like you."

"Did you want a horse for Maggie as well?" asked Giles.

"Nay," Evan answered. "She will ride with me. Now go."

"Aye, my lord." Giles ran off to do as told.

Daegel's soft chuckle made Evan turn back around. "What is so funny?" he asked.

"You are," said Daegel. "You are knocking yourself out trying to get the attention of a mere commoner, and you are making a fool of yourself doing it."

"Nay, I'm not. I am just offering my service to her. As a knight. It's my duty."

"Stop wasting your time," grunted Daegel. "It doesn't matter because it'll all be over in a few days anyway."

"I'm not wasting my time." Evan thought his cousin was talking about the fact that Maggie said she was leaving. "I highly intend to change the midwife's mind and convince her to stay right here at the castle instead of moving on."

"I'm not sure your betrothed will like that." Daegel got up and slipped his sword into his scabbard.

"What betrothed? I'm not betrothed."

"Not right now, you're not. But I heard our fathers talking. Uncle Garrett has set up an appointment this week for you to meet the wench."

"What are you saying? What wench?"

"Your bride-to-be, you fool! I didn't overhear her name or where she is from, but your father intends to have you betrothed in the next week, and married off as soon as the proper time for posting the wedding banns has passed."

"What?" This shocked Evan to hear this. He knew he'd be betrothed sooner or later, but was hoping for a little later. He'd just got knighted yesterday. And wedding banns were only posted for a mere three weeks before the wedding. He wanted to enjoy his new title a while before being tied down to a woman he didn't know. Alliances like these often didn't take the opinion of the groom-to-be into consideration, but still he wished his father had talked with him first. Evan didn't want an ugly or haughty bride. Neither did he want one who followed him around like a puppy and was afraid to speak her mind. Nay, after meeting Maggie he had a whole different idea about the kind of girl he'd like to be with, that's for sure. "I am not getting married. Not yet," said Evan.

"Whatever you say. Just don't let your father hear that, because word is that he's already sent out the missive and your prospective bride will be here any day now."

"Damn," muttered Evan under his breath, as he hurried

to the stables. Things were happening too fast all of a sudden. He could try talking to his father, but if he'd already made a betrothal arrangement for him with a baron or an earl, it was going to be hard to stop. Nobles made alliances for a purpose, and breaking a betrothal was not a good thing. Why hadn't his father talked to him first? Being Lord Warden, he often treated Evan like one of his men, giving orders without even considering that Evan might have a preference or something to say about the girl he was to marry.

Evan hurriedly made his way to the stables, to find Maggie about to get into a cart with a fishmonger who had delivered fish to the castle and was heading back to town.

"Maggie," he called out, stopping her just as she was about to crawl up to the bench seat of the wagon with the seedy-looking man. "What are you doing?"

"I found another way to get to town, so I won't need you to take me after all," she told him.

"Hold on," he said, walking over and looking at the man in the wagon. He was old and smelly and missing several teeth. His clothes were torn and filthy. And the worst part of it was that the man had a look of lust in his eyes. There was no way Evan would allow Maggie to be alone with this man, who would most likely accost her as soon as they rode out the gate. "Go, Fishmonger," he instructed. "The girl won't be riding with you, after all."

The old man scowled but obeyed, leaving the courtyard without Maggie.

"Why did you do that?" she spat.

"I did it because there was no doubt in my mind that as soon as you left the castle, he'd try to abduct you."

"And why do you care?"

Evan let out a deep sigh. "Maggie, I am trying to help you but you keep pushing me away. Why?"

"I don't need your help." She slipped the basket over her arm and started heading for the gate. He followed.

"You do need my help and you know it. For instance, in those dirty clothes and shoes that show your toes, no one is going to respect you enough to give you a job. Now stop being so stubborn and come with me to the stable. I told you, I'll take you to town. We'll stop on the way and I'll buy you new clothes and shoes as well."

"I don't need your pity nor your generosity, but thank you. I'll be fine on my own," she said and kept on walking.

"My lord, here is your horse." Giles approached with Evan's horse saddled and ready to go. "Will you be wanting me to accompany you to town?" asked the boy.

"Nay," said Evan hoisting himself atop his horse. He wanted to be alone with Maggie. Then again, he didn't want the wench making up a lie that he tried to abduct her or something. And with this one, he wasn't sure what she was going to do next. Mayhap it was a good idea to have Giles along as a witness just in case the girl tried to start trouble. He turned his horse in a circle and looked back to Giles. "I've changed my mind. Get your horse and follow me, but keep your distance. Just keep a close watch."

"Oh. All right," said Giles. "What about the midwife?" He craned his neck and looked across the courtyard as Maggie walked quickly to the front gate. "Is she coming with us?"

"Aye. She'll ride with me, but stay close and watch her every action."

"I am confused, Sir Evan." Giles scratched his head. "For what exactly will I be watching?"

Evan looked over at the girl when he answered. "Keep an open eye for any games that girl decides to play, because I am not in a sporting mood today."

CHAPTER 5

Maggie hightailed it for the gate, hoping to get out of the castle and to the road before Evan started after her. She had almost made it out of the castle before he showed up, but then he'd pulled her away from the fishmonger at the last moment. Actually, she had been a little leery of climbing into the wagon with that filthy, scary man, so mayhap this was for the best. She'd just keep her eyes open for a traveler with a wagon on the road who seemed safe, and ask them for a ride to town instead.

She was almost over the drawbridge when she hear the clip-clop of a horse's hooves coming up behind her. It was getting faster and she realized it was probably a guard or a noble so she moved to the side, hoping not to be trampled. The horse and rider came up behind her before she could even turn to look. She screamed when a man's hands reached down from his horse and he grabbed her, swinging her up into the saddle with him.

"Nay! Leave me alone," she screamed, her hair in her eyes so she wasn't able to see her abductor. If she hadn't been gripping her basket with two hands trying not to lose her belongings, she would have reached out and slugged him.

"Stop squirming or we're both going to end up on the ground," the man commanded in a deep voice.

She pushed her hair from her eyes to see that she was on her belly and flung across the lap of a man, riding atop a horse with none other than Evan. His hand on her back steadied her as her body pressed against his and her feet dangled off the side.

"Oh. It's you," she said, letting out a frustrated breath. "You almost made me dump my basket." She struggled to get to an upright sitting position in the saddle.

"You're welcome," he said, helping her. The rich timbre of his voice resonated against her back as she faced forward.

"I wasn't thanking you."

"I know. But deep in your heart I am sure you are grateful that I saved you from being molested by a toothless, filthy, lusty old man who smells like the rotting flesh of week-old fish. I must point out that I just came from the practice field, so I cannot vouch for the fact I smell much better at the moment. Still, at least I have all my teeth, so I'm not half as scary."

His words amused her and suddenly things didn't seem so grim anymore. Something about being with Evan made her heart sing. She smiled. "I think even your sweat smells sweeter than that fishmonger's rancid breath!"

They both laughed at that.

"You might want to move a little closer to me so you don't fall off the horse. Lean back against me and I'll put my arm around you if you'd like."

"Oh," she said, feeling her heartbeat picking up in speed. She shimmied her butt closer to him, sliding in between his spread legs. Maggie was reluctant to let him put his arm around her, so she refrained from leaning back against him. It felt much too intimate to do so. She didn't even know this man. "I'd better sit upright and hold on to my basket. I don't want to lose anything important."

"I'd say you're more important than anything you could possibly have in there." He nodded at the basket. "But don't worry. I'll hold on to you anyway and I promise I won't let you fall." Evan snaked one hand around her waist, drawing her tightly against him.

It felt damned good to Maggie. She hadn't been touched by a man since the death of her husband just after she had gotten pregnant with Emma. Evan's strong arm around her felt so protective. She instantly relaxed in his embrace. An odd feeling of being safe washed through her. Feeling safe was something that she had not felt in a long time now.

"Thank you," she whispered, and he heard her.

"There is no need to thank me, Midwife. I am just doing my job."

Somehow she felt he was calling her Midwife instead of by her name and also saying he was just doing his job because she'd told him the same thing when he'd tried to thank her for helping Lady Martine.

"Oh, I see your squire following us," she said, looking back at the road as they traveled.

"Yes, I asked Giles to accompany us."

"I see. I'm sure it is safer to have him to protect you since you'll be carrying a lot of money on your return from collecting all those taxes."

He laughed heartily at that. Maggie felt his chest rumble.

"What is so amusing?" she asked.

"I don't need anyone to protect me," he told her. "Besides, my squire is still in training and has a long way to go before I can count on him to have my back."

"Then why did you ask him to accompany you?" she asked out of curiosity.

"It was for your protection, Maggie."

"I don't understand." She turned her head to look into his clear green eyes. "You are a knight, Sir Evan. I thought you were going to protect me."

"I am. But let's just say ... he is going to protect you from me."

"What?" Her body stiffened. Did he mean to hurt her after all? Or since he said he'd buy her clothes, was he planning on getting her naked and taking advantage of her? Right now, she didn't know what to think.

"Relax, Maggie. I am not going to harm you nor take advantage of you," he said, almost as if he had heard her thoughts. "I just meant he is here as a witness."

"A witness? To what?" She still wasn't able to relax.

"To whatever might happen, or more likely whatever someone might accuse me of, even though it isn't true."

It took her a minute to know what he meant, but finally it dawned on her. He thought she was going to accuse him of doing something, even though the thought had never entered her mind. "Sir Knight, I am disappointed that you'd think I would accuse you of improper behavior between us. That is what you mean, is it not?"

Evan could have kicked himself for saying what he did. He didn't want her to think he was a lustful cur, but in defending himself from something that never even had the chance to happen, he'd more or less insinuated that she might be a liar.

"I didn't mean you'd make up anything. I just meant ... I mean ..."

"It's all right," she said, surprising him that she no longer sounded angry. "I am sure that being a noble you need to take every measure to protect your reputation."

"Well, I suppose," he said, not meaning that at all. Still, anything he said would probably just make the situation worse, and he was trying to get the girl to like him. He decided to just keep his mouth shut for now.

They traveled in silence until they got to town. He stopped and dismounted, holding his arms up to aid her.

He half expected her to slap away his hands or to dismount on her own but she didn't. Instead, she reached out with her arm still through the basket handle, and put her hands on his shoulders. With his hands encircling her waist, he gently lifted her from the horse, slowly sliding her down his body until her feet touched the ground.

Damn, he liked the feel of her small waist under his fingers. He liked even more the way her curves pushed out from under her clothes. Never had he thought a wench dressed in mainly rags could excite him. Maggie's clothes were dirty, but her body smelled heavenly. Like she'd used some kind of sweet herb on her hair and skin.

"Mmm, you smell good," he said, already regretting saying this aloud.

"What you are smelling is one of the medicinal oils I make. This one is infused with honeysuckle."

"Honeysuckle? Like the flower?" he asked, slowly removing his hands from her waist.

"Yes. The flower. Exactly. It is good for lots of things." She put her basket on the ground and fixed her head wrapping, tucking her hair beneath the covering, since it had all become exposed during their little escapade on the road.

"It is? I didn't know that. Like what?"

"Well, honeysuckle is used to fight inflammation, infections, and it even aids digestion. I use it when I wash my hair because it keeps my hair healthy."

"You have beautiful hair," he said, so mesmerized by the woman that he couldn't stop himself from reaching out and tucking a silky strand of her light blonde hair behind her ear. He noticed the way her face reddened and her gaze dropped to the ground when he did it. He cleared his throat and quickly pulled back his hand when he noticed his squire atop his horse watching them. "So. What else is honeysuckle good for?" asked Evan.

"Actually, infused in hot water it makes a good drink to help with nausea during pregnancy," she explained. "I want to make the drink for Lady Martine, but I don't have any more dried honeysuckle flowers. I had hoped to either purchase some in town today or pick the flowers myself, if I can find them growing nearby."

"What do they look like?" he asked her.

"There are several different kinds, but the type I believe will be blooming now is the climbing one. They are trumpet-shaped flowers with a sweet essence, and they're usually yellow or white."

"They climb? Like on a vine against a building?" he asked.

"Yes, that's right."

"Ah, I think I know exactly where to find them. There is a vine like that that is growing up the side of the blacksmith's shop in town. I know the smith well. His name is Alan. I will ask him when I collect his rent if he'd mind if you picked some of the flowers."

"Thank you," she told him. "I would like that."

Maggie strapped on her new shoes, picking up the hem of her new gown to take a better look at them. Evan had brought her to a mercantile that sold a few simple gowns for women, and then to the cordwainer's shop where he insisted on getting her shoes to go with her new gown. He'd also made sure to leave her old gown and holey shoes behind. Maggie actually felt better already. It was amazing how clean clothes and a good pair of shoes could change her mood so quickly, giving her a dose of confidence. Now she felt like she was ready to face anyone and not only ask for a job, but get it, too.

"Why don't you join me in collecting the rents today?" Evan asked her, as they left the cordwainer's shop.

"No, thank you. I don't think I'd like that." The thought of assisting a noble as he took hard-earned money away from a working commoner just didn't sit right with her.

"Are you sure?" he asked. "It would be a new experience for you, I'm sure."

"Nay," she said once again. "I have several supplies that I am hoping to find so I will know where to refill them once I get a job and have money again, but thank you for offering."

"Oh, that reminds me." Evan untied a small pouch of coins from his belt and tossed it to his squire still sitting atop his horse. "Giles, take this and purchase whatever supplies Maggie needs."

"Nay! I can't take your money," Maggie objected.

"Why not?" he asked. "I have plenty of it."

"I'm sure you do. However, you've already been kind enough to buy me a gown and shoes, and this is really too much."

"Consider the clothes a gift. And the bag of coins is your pay for helping my cousin."

Maggie eyed the heavy bag of coins Giles tossed up and down in his hand. Giles smiled as the clanking noise filled the air. "My lord, I have only worked for you for a day," she pointed out. My fees are high, but I assure you that you have overpaid me threefold."

"Then consider it an advance on your pay." Evan climbed atop his horse, not seeming at all concerned about this.

"Are you ready to go, Maggie?" asked Giles, tying the money pouch to his belt.

"Not yet." She removed her apron from her bag and put it over her new gown. Then, having had to remove her cap earlier when she dressed in her new gown, she replaced that as well.

"Why are you wearing your midwife cap and apron over your new gown?" Evan asked her from atop his horse.

"I thought it couldn't hurt," she said with a shrug. "Some people don't believe I'm a midwife since I am so young, but seeing me dressed like one might lessen their doubt."

"How old are you, anyway?" he asked.

"I am twenty."

"I am one-and-twenty," he said. "So, you have just one child?"

"Yes. I gave birth to Emma when I was sixteen."

"You said you are a widow, so you don't have a husband, then." Evan wanted to find out more about Maggie, and she was finally starting to talk. He was extremely curious about her parents and husband and if she had any siblings.

"Nay, I don't. That is usually what being a widow means."

"Yes, I know that. So, what happened to Emma's father?"

"He died in a fishing accident in a storm just after we were married."

"Oh. Sorry to hear that," he said, meaning it sincerely. "Do you have any other siblings? Besides Charles?"

"Nay. Just Charles. And before you ask, my father died from a passing pestilence when I was only thirteen."

"What about your mother?"

Maggie's head snapped up and she suddenly seemed to become guarded.

"What about her?"

"How did she die?"

It seemed to strike a nerve in Maggie that he'd asked, even though she had volunteered the information freely about the death of her father. Her body suddenly became rigid and she clenched her jaw. "She's dead, and that is all that matters, my lord," she said, reaching down and picking up her basket.

"I know she's gone. I was just curious how it happened, that's all."

Her expression became even colder. "Sir Evan, I really need to inquire about a job, find and replenish my supplies, and get back to the castle to check on Lady Martine, all in a timely manner. I am sure you are anxious to collect your rents as well."

"Yes. I suppose we should get back to business, if that's what you mean."

"I will meet you at the blacksmith's shop later." She started to walk away.

"Wait, Maggie," he called out. "Be sure to stay with Giles. He is escorting you today. Giles, keep a good eye on her and don't leave her side."

"Aye, my lord," said Giles, hopping down from his horse. "You can count on me. Maggie, did you want to ride on my horse with me?" asked the boy, seeming much too happy of the possible prospect of having a pretty woman in his arms atop his steed.

"That is sweet of you to ask, Giles. However, I prefer to walk, but thank you," said Maggie, making her way down the wooden walkway in front of the shops, not waiting for a man to escort her. Then again, it sounded as if Maggie hadn't really had a man in her life besides her brother in a long time now.

Evan decided he would have to take care of that, because a strange voice inside his head said not to share Maggie with anyone. Aye, he wanted to be the only man in her life for right now, and he was going to make it happen.

CHAPTER 6

Maggie was able to easily find most of the supplies she needed, but still felt guilty purchasing them with Evan's money. As soon as she found permanent work, she'd be sure to repay him. She'd spent the last two hours going from shop to shop, inquiring about possibly getting a job as a midwife here in town and asking if anyone could help her.

People weren't very friendly to a stranger and shrugged her off, not willing to give her any information. Finally, in the last place she'd gone, she'd gotten her answer, although it wasn't the one she was hoping for.

"My good friend Gunnora is the midwife in this town, as well as at Saltwood Castle," said the wife of the baker. She was a hefty woman, with double chins and chunky arms that looked like tree trunks.

"Oh, is Gunnora the midwife who is out of town helping a family member?" asked Maggie, as politely as she could.

"That's right. What of it?" The woman's hands went to

her hips and she looked like she was getting ready for battle. "You trying to steal her job, or what?"

"Steal her job?" repeated Maggie. "Nay, of course not." She forced a smile, trying to get the woman to smile too, but it wasn't working. Even though Maggie wanted to turn and run right now, she stayed and tried to be as pleasant as she could. Mayhap that would help soften this woman's bad disposition.

The bells to the bakery shop jangled as Giles walked in. He had been waiting outside for her at Maggie's request. She thought people might be leery of her if she applied for a job with a knight's squire looking over her shoulder.

"Maggie, are you almost ready? Sir Evan is expecting us at the smithy, and I am sure you are anxious to get back to aid Lady Martine with her pregnancy," said Giles.

The baker woman's mood got even worse at hearing Giles say this. "So, you are already working as a midwife at the castle. You did steal Gunnora's job, like I thought." The massive female made her way around the counter with a large wooden rolling pin clutched in one hand. Her other hand went to her waist. Maggie wasn't sure that the woman wasn't going to try to hit her.

"Nay, you've got it wrong," said Maggie, clutching her basket and taking a step backward. "I am only helping out until Gunnora returns, I promise. I am looking for a job but I am not trying to steal a job from another midwife."

"Well, I think you are and I don't like it." When the woman got closer Maggie noticed the hair growing on the woman's chin which only made her look even meaner. A bad feeling twisted in Maggie's gut and all she wanted to do right now was to go, but her feet seemed to be stuck to the ground. Her fear kept her from moving. "If you don't leave town at once and stop trying to steal my friend's job, I'm going to make you sorry." The baker raised her rolling pin in the air. Maggie stepped back so abruptly that she knocked into Giles and fell to the ground, landing on her butt.

Giles quickly pulled his sword and held it under the woman's chin. "Leave her alone or I'll have to teach you a lesson," he threatened.

The woman slowly lowered the rolling pin. "Who the hell are you?"

"I am the squire of Sir Evan Blackmore, and I promise you he'll hear all about the way you are treating his girl."

"His girl?" Maggie mumbled, surprised to hear this. Shocked, actually. Is that what Evan told his squire about her? If so, it meant that Evan liked her. Impossible. He was a noble and she was naught but a common midwife.

"You're a squire?" The woman squinted at Giles and cocked her head. "Nay, you're not. I recognize you now. You're that milksop page from the castle who is afraid of his own shadow." She laughed heartily. "You probably don't even know how to use that big blade, let alone hold it properly. I warn you that I am faster with my rolling pin than you will ever be with that sword. You are just a scared boy pretending to be brave, and we both know you will never amount to anything."

"Nay, Thomasina. Stop!" called out the baker's husband, running in from the other room. "Please, you must forgive my wife." He was a small man, and his huge wife towered over him. Maggie almost laughed aloud because these two didn't seem to belong together. The man held up a pouch that was clutched in his fingers. It was a black leather bag with a loaf of bread painted on the front of it. "I think when Sir Evan collected the rent earlier my wife forgot to give him all of it." He handed over the pouch of coins to Giles. "Please, take this to your lord. And please don't mention my wife's brash behavior to Sir Evan. We wouldn't want to upset him."

"Nay, I don't suppose so." Giles took the coin pouch and lowered his sword. He reached down and helped Maggie to her feet. "Just don't let it happen again," warned Giles, escorting Maggie to the door and not turning his back on the baker and his wife until he was outside.

"My, you were fierce in there," said Maggie, as soon as they got outside. "Thank you for protecting me, Squire." She turned to see the boy sweating profusely. His face was as white as snow and she wasn't sure he wouldn't faint. She swore she saw his body shaking. "Giles? Are you all right?"

"I think so," he said, sheathing his sword and handing her the pouch of coins that the baker man had given him. "Here, Maggie, you take this. Use the money to buy more supplies."

"Nay, I can't do that," she said, looking at the pouch, rubbing her thumb over the white loaf of bread painted on the leather. "It wouldn't be right. The baker said that this is part of the rent due." She held it back out to Giles.

"It's not," Giles assured her, pushing the bag of coins away from him.

"How do you know that?" asked Maggie.

"Sir Evan would never leave the shop without first counting all the rent money to make sure it was all there. If not, he would be sure to get it. This is naught but a bribe for me to keep my mouth shut and not tell Sir Evan about his wife's awful behavior."

"Oh, I see." She tested the weight of the coin pouch in her hand. It felt like more money than she'd had in a long while. "I still think that mayhap you should give this to Sir Evan."

"I can't," said Giles. "If I do, he'll ask what it is for."

"Mayhap you should tell him. After all, that woman was horrible and even threatened us." She looked up to see the baker's wife spying at them out the window of her shop.

"Maggie, please. I'd rather forget all about this if you don't mind."

"Why? I don't understand."

Giles let out a deep breath, looked around, and then lowered his head, speaking softly to Maggie. "Because what the woman said is true. I'm not brave. I really am a coward just like she said. Oh, Maggie, I don't want Sir Evan to know it. Please, don't tell him."

"Of course not." Her heart went out to the boy. He still seemed shaken and it was from confronting a woman!

"Put the coin pouch away before someone sees it and tries to steal it." Giles looked up and down the street. "This isn't the best part of town, and robberies happen often. We need to be alert and careful."

"If you're sure," she said, quickly peeking into the bag of coins. Her jaw dropped open. There would be enough money here to not only replenish her linens and herbs, but to also feed and take care of Charles and Emma for at least the next month or two. This would come in quite handy while she was trying to find a steady job.

"We'd better get to the smithy," said Giles, blowing out

another big breath of air, seeming as if he were trying to calm his nerves. "Sir Evan won't like us being late."

"Yes, of course," said Maggie, slipping the bag of coins into her basket.

"It might be wise not to mention this incident to Sir Evan," Giles reminded her once again.

"Are you sure?" she asked. "It seems to me he should know."

"My nerves are still a little shaken," Giles admitted. "You see, I've never had a confrontation with anyone before. If we have to go back to the bakery with Sir Evan, I'm afraid I might not be able to keep my composure around that frightening woman."

"Giles? Are you sure you're all right?" asked Maggie with a smile. She couldn't believe that a squire of a knight could be so nervous and afraid of a woman. Shouldn't he have confidence and be able to protect his liege lord?

"Maggie, can I be honest with you?" asked Giles, holding the reins of his horse as they headed down the street to the blacksmith's shop.

"Of course, you can. What is it?"

"I never wanted to be a squire, but because I come from a noble family it is required of me. I don't really like it and I'm not even sure I have the ability. I'll never really be able to do the job."

"Yes, you will," she said, gently reaching out and resting her hand on his arm.

"I'm no good at it and will never be. Just like the baker's wife said."

"I don't believe that, Giles. You were quite brave in there just now, protecting me. I am sure when the time comes to protect Sir Evan, you will do just as well. And I'm sure in time you will love being a squire. It just takes a long while to train, so be patient and stop being so critical of yourself."

"I hope you're right," he told her. "Because I'm afraid the first time I follow Sir Evan into battle that I'll die. I really don't want to die."

"No one wants you to die, Giles," she told him in a kind voice. "You worry too much. Just have confidence in yourself and you'll be fine. I saw you stand up to that awful woman in there and I was very impressed by your actions."

"You were?" he asked her, seeming more than surprised that she said this.

"Yes. I thought you were very brave and just as fierce as that madwoman. After all, you not only protected me but got the woman's husband to pay you just to keep the secret. You are very good at being a squire indeed."

"Thank you," said Giles, standing a little taller. "Mayhap I am just too critical with myself like you say. I'll try to have more confidence. I don't want to let Sir Evan down. Ever."

Evan paced the floor of the smithy, wondering what in the world was taking Giles and Maggie so long to get there. They should have been here to meet him a half-hour ago. Peering out the window of the shop, he finally saw them coming up the walkway. They were walking side by side, and Giles held on to the reins of his horse as the animal followed. To Evan's surprise, Maggie had her hand on Giles's arm. They were both smiling and laughing.

Jealousy reared its ugly head. Hell, she hadn't even held

Evan's arm when he escorted her. And she was smiling more with Giles than she had with him since he'd met her.

"What'cha lookin' at?" asked the smithy, wiping the sweat from his brow and pumping the bellows to feed the fire in the forge.

"Nothing, Alan." Evan hurried back to a small table with a lock and keys on it. He'd had an interest in locks and keys his whole life. As a youth he had come to town often to visit the blacksmith who was also a locksmith. Alan saw he'd had an interest and started teaching Evan how to repair locks. Soon, Evan started making keys in the forge and designing locks that hung on chests, too. It was a creative thing to do that took him away from his troubles and worries. He focused on the lock he'd been trying to repair and the new key he'd made for it over the past year. As an adult it was getting harder and harder to pursue this interest, since as a noble, he shouldn't be spending time at the town smithy. As a knight, he'd be lucky to ever get back to the craft. Then again, nobles weren't craftsmen—or at least they weren't supposed to be.

Giles and Maggie entered the shop.

"My, it is dark in here," Maggie's sweet voice floated in the thick and ashen air. She coughed. "It is a little hard to breathe. And hot."

"This is no place for a lady." Evan got to his feet. "Maggie, this is my friend, Alan. He said you are welcome to harvest the honeysuckle that is climbing up the outside of his building."

"Thank you," said Maggie, her eyes going to the lock and key on the table. "What are you doing?" she asked, walking over to inspect it.

"It's nothing," he said, brushing off his hands. "I just like tinkering with locks."

"This is very good work." She picked up the lock and key and inspected it. "You made this key in the forge, didn't you," she asked, turning it over to inspect it. "You did a good job heating and hammering out the shank, and were precise with the files making the ward."

"That's right," said Evan. "How do you know about that?"

"My father was a locksmith," she told him, placing the key back down on the table. "My little brother and I used to go to work with Father sometimes when we were children, while Mother was assisting with a birth. I was supposed to be watching Charles, but I found more interest in watching my father make and fix locks. Actually, Charles was even more interested in the craft than I was. My father would put him on his lap to watch while he worked. He would even let him help once in a while and that meant the world to Charles."

"So you know a little about this, then."

"Oh, yes. I remember a little but I am not skilled at it, and neither do I want to be. It is my brother Charles who always wanted to be a locksmith and follow in my father's footsteps."

"Did I hear your brother is interested in being a locksmith?" Alan wiped his hands on a cloth and walked over to join them. "It just so happens that I am in need of an apprentice. Of course, he won't be paid, but he would gain a lot of experience working here. I would teach him everything he needs to know. If he makes it to journeyman someday, he can actually bring in good money knowing the trade.”

“That is a great offer,” Giles interrupted. “If I wasn’t a squire, I think I’d like to be a locksmith.” He walked over and picked up a lock and clicked it shut, causing Evan to groan.

“Giles, I don’t have the key for that lock finished yet,” Evan told him.

“Sorry,” said Giles with a shrug, then putting the lock back down.

“I’d like to meet your brother,” said Alan. “How old is he, and is he working anywhere right now?”

“Charles is not yet fourteen,” said Maggie. “And nay, he doesn’t have a job, although he’d like to.”

“He’s the perfect age to start his apprenticeship,” said Alan. “When can you bring him in?”

“I can’t,” she told him.

“Maggie, what are you saying?” asked Evan. “This is an opportunity of a lifetime. Charles shouldn’t pass it up.”

“We’d have to be living here in town for him to be an apprentice, and sadly, we’re not,” Maggie explained to Alan.

“Oh, really? So, where do you live?” asked the man.

“She’s living at the castle for now,” Evan answered for her.

“She is?” Alan sounded impressed. “You are a midwife for the nobles?” he asked, noticing her apron and cap.

“Nay, I’m not!” Maggie almost sounded angry. “It is a temporary position, but I and my family will be leaving soon. I was in town today to look for a job, but it seems there is no opening. No room for me here.”

“I’m sure you’d be a welcome breath of fresh air compared to that grumpy old midwife, Gunnora.” Alan chuckled. "If I were a pregnant woman, I'd be afraid to have the wench touch me." He faked a shudder.

"I won't be stealing anyone's job, if that is what you are insinuating," insisted Maggie. "Now, if you'll excuse me, I need to harvest the flowers before the dew sets in."

"I'll help you," offered Giles, opening the door and holding it for her. He left with Maggie, leaving Evan once again sitting alone.

Alan released a low whistle. "She's a looker, that one, and feisty too." His gaze was focused on Maggie out the door as she reached up to pick the flowers. "Know if she's available?"

"She's not," growled Evan, leaving the smithy and wishing now that he hadn't brought the girl to town after all.

CHAPTER 7

Maggie woke up the next morning, turning over on her pallet and realizing by the noise outside her door that it was already morning. It sounded as if the servants were working, clanking around dishes in the kitchen. She could smell the aroma of breakfast pottage and bacon, and her stomach growled.

"Emma, Charles, get up," she said, yawning and walking over to light a candle since the room had no windows and the room was dark. "We overslept." After lighting the tallow candle, she rubbed her eyes. "Charles? Emma?" They weren't in the room.

Thinking they were out roaming around the castle, she hurriedly dressed, once again putting on her gown and the midwife apron over it. She was afraid Charles might have let Emma wander off again. So instead of putting on her cap, she stuck it in her bag and slipped the bag over her shoulder. She shoved her feet into her shoes and pulled open the door.

"My basket," she said aloud, going back for her basket of

supplies. She needed to make a hot honeysuckle drink to bring up to Lady Martine this morning. Cursing herself for sleeping so late, she hoped that Lady Martine was not having any problems with her pregnancy. Then again, if she was, Maggie was sure someone would have sought her out by now. Grabbing her basket, she headed out into the kitchen, weaving her way between the servants until she got to the hearth. "May I have a cup of hot water, Lucy?" she asked the cook, whom she had befriended the other day. "It is for Lady Martine."

"Of course," said the old woman, fetching a wooden cup and ladling some hot water into it from a pot hanging over the fire. "I just prepared a tray of food to bring to Ladies Martine and Eleanor. I was about to bring it abovestairs for them."

"I can take it," Maggie offered.

"All right," said Lucy, ladling some pottage into a bowl and adding it to the tray with the covered dishes. "This is for you, Maggie. You need to eat to keep up your strength taking care of those two children."

"Speaking of the children, have you seen my daughter and my brother at all this morning?" Maggie looked around the kitchen but couldn't find them.

"Aye. They ate earlier with Sir Evan, and then they went somewhere with him."

"What?" Her head snapped upward. "What do you mean? God's eyes, don't tell me that Charles let Emma climb the dais and they sat down to eat with the nobles?"

"No, not at all," said the woman with a giggle. "But Sir Evan did sit right here in the kitchen and eat with them. Your little girl actually sat on his lap."

"Oh, please tell me this isn't so." Maggie felt as if she were starting to have chest pains. Her life shouldn't be so filled with stress the first thing in the morning. What was Sir Evan thinking? "Why was he eating with commoners?"

"I'm not sure," answered Lucy. "However, I overheard the boy and Sir Evan talking about locks or keys or something."

"He didn't. He wouldn't," said Maggie, afraid that Sir Evan had taken Charles and Emma into town to see his blacksmith friend, Alan. Mayhap she needed to go after them. She was about to do just that when Lady Martine's maidservant ran into the kitchen.

"Oh, Maggie, I'm so glad to find you. Lady Martine sent me to fetch you."

"I'm on my way. Carry this tray for me," she instructed the maidservant, reaching into her basket and grabbing a few honeysuckle flowers which she dropped into the cup of hot water. "Hurry," she said, picking up her bag and basket. "Lady Martine needs me."

Hurriedly making her way up the stairs, Maggie lost no time in getting to Lady Martine's room as quickly as possible. A quick knock, and Maggie opened the door and entered without even waiting to be granted access.

"I'm here," she cried. "How are you feeling, Lady Martine? I am so sorry that I overslept." Maggie stopped in her tracks when she saw the bed was empty. She spun around to find Martine sitting up in a chair. Evan sat in another chair across from his cousin, with Emma on his lap. Lady Eleanor wasn't there at the moment and neither did she see Charles. "What's all this?" asked Maggie in confusion. She hurried over to Lady Martine and pressed her hand against the lady's forehead. "You're not feverish, that's good."

"Nay, I'm not," Martine answered with a smile. "My stomach feels a little nauseous, but otherwise I am fine. I was tired of lying down, and Evan was kind enough to help me sit up."

"Then you're not in pain?" asked Maggie, trying to make sure everything was good.

"No. Not really." Martine was actually smiling. "But my babies are very active this morning. I even let your daughter feel my belly when they were both kicking at once." Martine put her hand on her belly and started to rub circles.

"I want a baby, Mama," said Emma, lying back against Evan's chest and kicking her feet in the air.

"No, you don't, sweetheart," she said, putting down her things. "Where is Charles? Why isn't he watching you?"

"I gave him some time off," Evan answered before Emma could answer. "I said I'd watch Emma for you so you could sleep late."

"I don't like to sleep late, and I don't want Charles off running about while a knight is playing nursemaid to my daughter."

"Nursemaid?" Evan made a dissatisfied expression. "I'd prefer if you never referred to me in that manner again."

"Sorry," said Maggie with her face turned downward, not having meant to insult a noble.

"Where shall I put the tray of food?" asked the handmaid, walking slowly so as not to spill anything.

"Put it down over here." Evan reached out and tapped the table next to him. "Something smells good." He picked up a lid and peered underneath. "Mmmm. Bacon, breakfast porridge, and fruit. How about something to eat, girls?"

"Oh, not yet," said Martine. "I can't even think of eating until the babies calm down and my stomach is soothed."

Maggie took the cup from the tray. "I have a drink to help you with that, my lady. It is hot water infused with honeysuckle flowers." Maggie picked up the cup and handed it to Martine. Martine peered inside curiously.

"Mmmm it smells and looks pretty," said Martine, blowing on the hot liquid. "I've never had this before." She took a sip and nodded. "It is delicious."

"Maggie picked the honeysuckle yesterday at the smithy," Evan told his cousin.

"Flowers are growing inside a blacksmith's shop?" Martine giggled.

"Nay, climbing up the wall outside," Evan corrected the conversation.

"Oh, is this the same blacksmith shop that Daegel took Charles to this morning?" asked Martine, taking another sip of the hot drink.

"Daegel took Charles to town? Why?" Maggie's gaze shot over to Evan. "Please don't tell me he is going there to talk with the blacksmith about Charles being his apprentice."

"No, he's not going there to talk about it," said Evan, making Maggie release a quick sigh of relief. But it didn't last long. "He's going there to start his first day of work," continued Evan. "You won't believe how excited Charles was when I told him he'd be learning to be a locksmith, just like his father."

Maggie was so angry at Evan right now that she was about to explode.

"What is this?" asked Emma, picking up a sweetmeat in her fingers from the food tray and sniffing it.

"That is candied fruit," Evan told her. "Try it."

"Mama, can I eat this?" asked Emma, her wide brown eyes looking up at Maggie, waiting for her approval.

"Emma, you already had food to break the fast." She looked over at Evan. "How could you do this? Without even talking to me first."

"I didn't think giving the children food earlier would upset you. They were hungry."

"That's not what I mean. I am talking about Charles and the apprenticeship."

"Emma, sweetheart," said Evan getting up and taking the little girl from his lap and setting her down on the chair. "Why don't you eat that sweetmeat while I talk to your mother in private."

"If you have something to say, then say it," demanded Maggie, crossing her arms over her chest.

"Perhaps you two could go into the wardrobe for a bit of privacy, while Emma and I enjoy our treats," suggested Martine, still sipping the honeysuckle water.

"Fine," said Maggie, not wanting to leave Emma. She stormed over to the adjoining room that was used to store clothes. Evan followed her into the small space. Lady Martine had gowns hanging up, and there were shelves holding shoes and extra hose and undergarments, too. There were more clothes and headpieces than Maggie had ever seen in her life. With barely any room to move, Maggie found herself standing toe-to-toe with Evan. "You knew I didn't want Charles to work in town, and yet you had your cousin bring him there. How could you?"

"Now, that's not fair, Maggie." Evan raised his hands in surrender. "You never said that to me, so how would I know?"

"You heard me tell Alan that I have no job and that we are not staying in Hythe."

"Yes, I heard you say it, but it's not true. You do have a job. Right here at the castle."

"You don't understand. I need a *permanent* job," she told him, feeling like he didn't listen to her at all. "Charles is not becoming an apprentice because we are not staying in Hythe."

"Maggie, relax. Everything will work out if you will just stop fighting it."

"I am not fighting it, I am—" Her words were cut off as Evan pulled her closer and covered her mouth with his. She started to push him away, but when he deepened the kiss and wrapped his strong arms around her, she felt herself melting into him.

Her eyes closed and her head fell back as he kissed her again, but this time with more passion. God's teeth, it felt wonderful to be kissed by a man. George had barely been more than a boy when she first married, and he wasn't even fond of kissing. To be kissed by Evan in this manner was something she'd never experienced before.

"That's better," he whispered, his breath hitting her wet lips, creating a sensuous tingle. "You have quite an extraordinary mouth. When it's used for kissing, instead of yelling at me."

"I enjoyed that," she admitted, still feeling like naught

more than clay in his hands. She was more than willing to let him mold her into anything he wanted her to be. "Kiss me again," she said, reaching up and putting her hands around his neck. Lost in the moment, Maggie forgot how angry she was with him.

"Gladly." They kissed again, and this time she felt him part her lips with his tongue. Then his tongue filled her mouth, and she thought she would die with elation because of the vibrant feelings that were coming alive inside her. She heard a moan of desire and to her surprise she realized it was coming from her!

They might have stayed there, kissing longer, but the loud rapping of someone's knuckles against the bedchamber door took their attention and they stopped.

"Come in," she heard Lady Martine call out, followed by a male voice.

"Martine, have you seen Evan? I cannot find him anywhere."

"It's my father," whispered Evan. He released Maggie and ran out into the bedchamber. Evan recognized the tone of concern in his father's voice. Something was wrong. "Father, I'm here. What it is?" he asked. Maggie followed him out of the wardrobe, looking down and running her tongue over her lips. She silently went over, picked up Emma, and stepped off to the back of the room, standing next to the maidservant.

"Evan?" His father, Garrett, narrowed his eyes. "What were you doing in the wardrobe with the midwife?"

"Uncle Garrett, you sounded as if something is wrong

when you came in," Martine thankfully interrupted. "What is it?"

"Evan, Martine, one of the king's messengers just arrived at the castle with some very disturbing news." Evan's father ran a weary hand over his hair.

"Tell us. What is it?" Evan wet his lips with his tongue, savoring the taste of Maggie, trying to still his heart and subdue his excitement after kissing her and having her return his kiss with such passion.

"The king is gone," he told them.

"Gone? Where did he go?" asked Martine.

"Nay, you don't understand." Garrett shook his head. "I am sorry to have to tell you two, but I've just received the news that King Edward III is dead."

CHAPTER 8

Evan paced the courtyard the next morning as his father, mother, and Lord Corbett got ready to leave with a traveling party to join other nobles and Barons of the Cinque Ports. They would gather together to mourn the king as they prepared to attend their ruler's funeral. His cousins Eleanor and Daegel were there, as well as his uncle, Brother Ruford. Maggie stood silently nearby with Charles and Emma as they watched what was happening.

"Father, let me come with you," begged Evan. "Please. I am a knight now, and should be there in respect of our deceased king."

"Nay," Garrett objected. "I need someone here to protect and maintain the castle until your mother and I return. Even though the king died in Surrey, he will most likely be buried at Westminster Abbey. We will have to travel with the other nobles. The preparations for the funeral might take a fort-night, so we will be gone at least that long."

Evan didn't like being left behind. If he was going to

follow in his father's footsteps and hopefully one day join the Confederation of the Cinque Ports, then he should be there at this crucial time with his father, other nobles, and the other Barons of the Cinque Ports.

"Can't Gar watch over things here while I join you?" he asked, speaking about his older brother.

"Nay, I need Gar with me. He can captain a ship better than anyone. With news of the king's death reaching across the channel, there is always a chance England will be attacked, being in this vulnerable state. I might even need to organize an extra fleet to patrol and protect the channel until the king's successor is crowned."

"Richard is just a child," said Eleanor, speaking about King Edward's nephew who was only ten. Since the Black Prince, Edward's eldest son, died last year, Edward's nephew was next in line for the throne.

"Yes, and that makes things even more complicated," stated Garrett. "There are many plans to make and decisions to consider. This is a very important time, and it is crucial I am there to participate, should I be needed."

"Evan," said his mother, coming up and taking ahold of Evan's arm. "I know you want to join us, but you are needed here, like your father said."

"I still don't see why I'm not traveling with you." Evan longed to join the others.

"One reason is because your betrothed will be arriving any day," answered his father, stunning Evan to hear this. "You need to stay here to greet her and her father."

"My betrothed," he repeated, his gaze shooting over to Maggie who looked up in surprise. Part of him didn't want Maggie to know. Not after the passionate kissing they'd done in the wardrobe yesterday. Ever since then Evan could think of nothing else but kissing Maggie again.

"See? It's just like I told you, Cousin," said Daegel from directly behind him, startling Evan and making him jump. Evan hadn't even known Daegel had moved closer.

"I'm sorry we haven't had time to discuss this, Son." Garrett mounted his horse. "But Brother Ruford knows all the details and he will fill you in on what to expect. I'm sorry, but we need to leave now. Echo, please hurry. You're going to make us late."

"I'm sorry," whispered Evan's mother, giving Evan a kiss on the cheek. "I tried to talk your father out of choosing a bride for you, but he insisted this was a good alliance and that it was the best thing for you."

"Mother, are you saying I don't even get to choose between several ladies?"

"Nay. Your father has already chosen for you."

"But I don't even have any information. Who is this girl? Where is she from? I know nothing about her."

"Echo, we've got to go," complained his father from atop his horse, sounding extremely anxious as well as irritated.

"I'm sure it will all work out, just give it time." Evan's mother cupped his cheek and smiled sweetly. "We'll see you soon. The castle is in your hands now. Daegel and Brother Ruford will be staying here also until our return. Oh, and take good care of Martine." She turned and walked away to join the traveling party.

Evan watched in sorrow as the entourage left the castle without him. He wished right now to be anywhere but here, waiting for his unknown betrothed to arrive. He always knew he'd someday be married to a noblewoman, but this was all so sudden. He'd just been knighted, and hadn't even had the time to think about his honorable position.

"Well, now what?" asked Daegel, crossing his arms over his chest as they watched the others leave. "Am I taking the boy back to town again today?"

"Nay," answered Evan. "Maggie doesn't want him to be an apprentice. Or at least not until she has a permanent job."

"I thought you took care of that."

"So did I. But she keeps insisting she will not steal the other midwife's job."

"All right. Then, I'm off to the practice yard. Want to join me?"

Evan turned to see Maggie, Charles, and Emma coming toward him.

"Nay, not now. Mayhap later," Evan told him, feeling like he needed to talk to Maggie.

"As Lady of the Castle now until my parents return, I'm afraid I won't be able to spend as much time in Martine's room with her," Eleanor told Evan.

"It's all right. I'll have Maggie stay there." Evan was about to tell Maggie that, when he heard someone call his name from behind him. He turned to see the castle steward standing there with two women.

"Pardon me, Sir Evan," said Stefan, stopping to speak to Evan. The women were right behind him. Evan recognized the fatter one as the wife of the baker from town. She always scowled at him when he collected the rent. Evan didn't tarry in the bakery since she wasn't the friendliest person, and he never knew what would happen if she was involved. The other woman he identified as Gunnora, the castle midwife.

"Yes, Stefan?" he asked, seeing Maggie, Charles, and Emma from the corner of his eye. His squire Giles was with them.

"It seems there is a problem."

"Well? What is it?" asked Evan, feeling as if his precious time were being wasted.

"I will let Gunnora tell you. Go on," the steward urged her to speak.

"My lord," said the old midwife, curtsying. She seemed unstable and Evan wasn't sure she wouldn't fall over. The baker's wife, whose name he couldn't remember, tried her best to curtsy as well.

"Midwife, I see you've returned," said Evan. "How is your family member?"

"She is close to dying," relayed the midwife.

"I see. Well, take off as much time as you need." Evan waved his hand through the air. "I have Maggie here, and she is tending to the midwife duties for now, so you needn't worry. She is doing a fine job." He looked over at Maggie and smiled.

"Actually, she is exactly whom this is all about," said Gunnora with a stiff upper lip.

"I am not trying to steal your job," Maggie spoke up, holding her daughter in her arms. "I was only here temporarily until you returned."

"Hmph," sniffed the midwife. "I sincerely doubt that is true, since my good friend here, Thomasina, tells me that the girl is a thief."

"What?" both Maggie and Evan said together.

"That is right, my lord." Thomasina looked over at Maggie and glared at her. "When she and that boy that you call your squire were in my shop the other day, she stole a money pouch from my husband."

"What?" gasped Maggie.

"That is a serious accusation," Evan warned the woman. "Think hard and long before you go calling Maggie a thief."

"It's true," said Thomasina. "I saw her put the money pouch in that basket she's carrying. If you look inside, I'm sure you'll find it."

"Maggie?" Evan looked over to her. "Is this true? Did you steal money from this woman and her husband? And if so, why?"

Before Maggie answered, she looked over at Giles. Giles seemed to become pale, dropping his gaze to the ground.

"Nay. I did not," stated Maggie with conviction.

"She's lyin'!" screamed the baker woman. "Check her basket. I'm sure you'll find out the truth."

Evan let out a deep sigh and walked over to Maggie. "I'm sorry," he said softly. "But as lord of the castle, I need to settle disputes. I will take a look in your basket, and then send the woman on her way when I prove that she is wrong." He dug his hand into her basket, his fingers closing over a small pouch. "What's this?" He picked it up and looked at it. Checking inside the leather pouch he discovered a good amount of coins, and it was not the pouch of money that he'd given her.

"Yes. That's my husband's money pouch!" yelled the woman. "It has a loaf of bread painted on the front and that proves that it is from the bakery."

Evan ran his thumb over the painted loaf of bread on the front, looking over to Maggie once again. "Maggie? Can you explain this?"

Maggie gave her daughter to Charles. "Charles, please take Emma to play with the other children."

"Aye," said Charles, doing as told.

Once they were gone, Maggie looked over at Giles once again. Giles seemed nervous, shifting his weight from one foot to the other. Something was going on between these two but Evan didn't know what it could be.

"Giles? Can you confirm that you and Maggie went into the bakery two days ago?" asked Evan.

"I–I ..." Giles looked up at Thomasina and then down to the ground again. Evan noticed that Thomasina was glaring at his squire, pounding her one fist into her open hand.

"We were there," Maggie spoke up. "But Giles doesn't know anything about the pouch of coins."

"What?" Evan felt like she was lying. After all, he'd told the boy to keep a close eye on Maggie, and he hadn't reported anything odd to Evan. Surely, if Maggie had stolen something, Giles would have seen her do it. "What do you mean?"

"I went inside the bakery to inquire about any midwife jobs, but this woman told me her friend was a midwife and would be returning soon," said Maggie.

"That's right," grumbled Gunnora. "And I'm back now, so you're not needed."

"Then you're saying you stole the coin pouch?" asked Evan, not believing that Maggie would really do such a thing. She had morals. Maggie didn't want money he tried to give her, and neither did she want to steal anyone's job. Nay. There was no way he'd believe that Maggie stole anything, no matter what these women said.

Maggie looked over at Giles once again, but the boy just looked the other way.

"I did take it," said Maggie.

"See? I told you," snapped Thomasina. "The girl is nothing but a thief."

"Aye, she's a thief," shouted Gunnora. "Throw her in the dungeon or cut off her hand to punish her. It's only right."

"Wait a minute," said Maggie, raising her hand. "I said I took it, but I didn't steal it. I found it lying outside the shop and just ... picked it up, that's all."

"That's a lie!" screamed Thomasina.

"Didn't you think to ask if it belonged to the baker since there was a loaf of bread painted on it?" asked Evan suspiciously.

"I suppose I should have." Maggie looked over to Giles once more. He raised his head slightly. Evan noticed the squire's eyes were closed and his breathing had quickened. "However, Giles said we needed to hurry since we were supposed to meet you at the smithy and we were already late."

"Is that right, Giles?" Evan asked his squire, thinking the boy was acting odd and wanting to hear from him as well.

"I did say that to her, my lord, that's true," he answered.

"Then I think this is finished." Evan handed the pouch back to the baker woman. "Here. Take your money and go."

"What?" The woman glared at Evan now. "I'm sure she already used a good portion of the money."

"I didn't use a penny," said Maggie. "Sir Evan, if you don't believe me you can ask the woman's husband. I'm sure he'll tell you how much was in the pouch."

"Nay, never mind. It's fine," grumbled Thomasina,

shoving the coin pouch into her bag. "You are not going to punish the thief, my lord?"

"Why should I?" asked Evan. "Maggie didn't steal anything."

"She stole my job," said Gunnora. "I don't like that. She needs to go."

"Maggie is not going anywhere," Evan told them.

"Don't worry, I am leaving today," Maggie assured the women.

"What?" Evan looked over at Maggie, shaking his head. "Nay, Maggie. You don't have to leave."

"I said that I'd stay until Gunnora returned and now she has." Maggie kept her calm composure, impressing Evan with her level of professionalism. "Gunnora, please take good care of Lady Martine. She is on bed rest because she will be birthing twins any day now."

"Twins?" The midwife looked up and wrinkled her nose. "Nay, that's not true. You don't know what you're sayin.' She's not havin' her baby for another month yet. One baby, mind you."

Maggie felt as if she were going to explode with anger if she didn't get away from there soon. These two women were horrible people and she wanted nothing to do with them.

"If you'll excuse me, my lord, I'll go pack and leave with my family right away." Maggie took off without waiting to hear Evan's answer.

She got to her room, wanting to throw herself down on the pallet and cry, but she wouldn't. She couldn't. It was important to stay strong. For Emma and Charles.

Blinking away her tears, she started to put their clothes and belongings into the travel bag. There was a small knock at the door and Evan stuck his head into the room.

"Maggie? Can we talk?"

"There is nothing to say." She continued to pack. "I will be out of here in the next hour and will no longer create problems for you."

"You don't create problems." He entered the room and closed the door behind him.

Her heart stilled. "Are you sure you should be in here with me with the door closed, my lord? What will people say?"

"I don't care what anyone says. I'll do what I want." Evan slowly walked over to Maggie, laying his hand on her shoulder. "Why did you lie about the money pouch?"

"What?" She froze, not wanting to face him.

"I know you are not a thief. If so, you wouldn't have given up your job to Gunnora so easily."

"I told you from the beginning I would leave when the midwife returned."

He put both his hands on her shoulders and slowly turned her around. "I know you were only trying to protect Giles."

"Whatever do you mean?"

"I saw the way you two exchanged glances and how nervous Giles became."

"Giles is not a thief, if that is what you are saying."

"Nay. I am not saying that at all. However, I know that awful Thomasina and how she threatens everyone. Did you know that her husband pays off people all the time to keep word from getting out that his wife has threatened them?"

"Oh. You know about that?" She looked up and blinked away a tear.

"I know," he said, gently reaching up and wiping away the tear with his thumb. "And I will bet anything that her husband paid Giles that money to keep quiet after his wife threatened him."

"Actually, he paid Giles after Thomasina threatened me."

"She did? Damn, I never should have let her walk out of here. Why didn't you tell me this sooner?"

"It doesn't matter." She tried to turn back to her packing, but Evan took her arm to stop her.

"Maggie, I know that Giles has a lot of fears and that he isn't the best choice of a squire."

"You do?" This surprised her that he knew. "Then why did you choose him as your squire?"

"Giles's father is a good friend of my father. My father and I are trying to help out Giles's family by training the boy to be a good squire, and to rid himself of his, shall we say, *girly* lack of courage."

Maggie smiled. "Girly? I'd hardly call Thomasina's overabundant amount of courage *girly*."

"I'd hardly call the woman a girl," he answered, and the tension broke when they both started laughing.

"Are you going to say anything to Giles?" she asked.

"Nay. Not now. I have faith that the boy will come around. He just needs to build his confidence a bit first."

"I will say that he was very brave when he drew his sword and protected me in the bakery."

"He did?" Evan nodded as if he were satisfied. "Then my plan is already working."

"Sir Evan, do you think it is wise to keep Giles as your squire?" asked Maggie. "I mean, he is supposed to be able to protect you on the battlefield."

"Believe me, Giles is not getting anywhere near a battlefield until I feel he is ready. I assure you that you have nothing to worry about regarding that."

"All right then. I'm glad to hear it. Well, I suppose I'd better finish packing."

"I don't want you to go, Maggie." Evan pulled her back into his arms and kissed her.

Maggie wanted to enjoy the kiss, but something was weighing heavy on her mind. She pulled away. "Sir Evan, you are betrothed and should not be kissing me," she said, although the thought of him never kissing her again about broke her heart.

"Evan," he said.

"What?" She blinked several times in succession.

"When we are alone, I want you to always call me Evan. Not *my lord* and not *Sir Evan*."

"But that wouldn't be right."

"I'll decide what is right and what is not." They kissed again, and although she meant to pull away, she had the hardest time doing it. She figured if this was the last kiss she'd ever get from Evan, then she wanted it to linger so she could enjoy it.

"Maggie, are you in there?" There came a quick knock and then the door swung open wide and Daegel entered the room. Maggie quickly pushed away from Evan, but Daegel had seen them kissing. "Oh, I'm sorry to interrupt." He smiled widely.

• • •

"Daegel, get that dung-eating grin off your face and tell me why the hell you are barging into Maggie's room, because I don't like it." Evan had been enjoying his time alone with Maggie, but his crazy cousin put a fast stop to that.

"It's Martine," said Daegel, looking at Maggie and still smiling.

"What about her?" asked Maggie, sounding concerned. "Is she all right?"

"I don't know," said Daegel with a shrug. "Her handmaid stopped me in the corridor saying she was looking for you. That Martine was summoning you."

"I'm sorry, but I am not the midwife here anymore," Maggie told him, feeling a stab to her heart since she cared about Lady Martine and really wanted to go to her chamber. "You should find the other midwife, Gunnora."

"Did you find her, my lord?" The handmaid ran up to the door, looking terrified. "Oh, Maggie, thank goodness you didn't leave yet. Gunnora said you were leaving for good but you can't! Lady Martine needs you."

"I'm sorry, but Gunnora will tend to her needs now," said Maggie. "She is the midwife here and it is her responsibility."

"Nay, you need to come to the bedchamber right away." The handmaid wouldn't stop.

"Why is that? Can't you find Gunnora?" Maggie's brow furrowed.

"The old midwife is in the bedchamber right now but she doesn't know what to do."

"What do you mean?" asked Maggie, concern showing on her face now. "She doesn't know what to do about what?"

"I can't find Lady Eleanor either," cried the handmaid. "I ran to get you because I am so frightened for her."

"It's all right. All will be fine," said Maggie calmly, taking the handmaid's hands in hers. "Now, please tell me why Lady Martine is calling for me."

"She's in pain. Lots of pain." The servant's eyes opened wide. "And she's bleeding!"

"Bleeding?" asked Maggie. "That's not a good sign."

"Are you sure about this?" Evan asked the girl.

"Yes, my lord," said the handmaid. "It almost seems as if Lady Martine is having her babies!"

CHAPTER 9

Evan groaned, not believing that this day could turn any worse, but suddenly it had. As if the problem with the baker's wife wasn't bad enough, now his cousin was having her babies, and by the sound of it, the castle midwife wasn't experienced enough to help Martine.

"Maggie, get your basket and get up to Lady Martine's room immediately," commanded Evan. "Handmaid, go with her and aid her however you can."

"Of course, right away," agreed Maggie. "I'll need extra linens and some hot water from the kitchen though."

"Handmaid, get it," ordered Evan.

"Yes, my lord," said the handmaid, rushing off to do as told.

"What about Gunnora?" asked Maggie, collecting the supplies she'd need. "She won't be happy if I barge in there and take over."

"Don't worry about that old she-goat. I am coming too, and I will put her in her place if need be." Evan headed for the door. "If my cousin's life is in peril I want you at her feet, not Gunnora."

"What can I do?" asked Daegel.

"Maggie, let us know," said Evan.

"Sir Daegel, can you find Charles and Emma and tell them to stay put in the great hall while I am helping Lady Martine?" asked Maggie. "Tell them it might be a while."

"Sure," said Daegel. "I'll make certain they get something to eat as well."

"Thank you." Maggie tied her apron around her, and quickly put her cap on her head and tucked her hair under the band.

"Find Eleanor too, Daegel," said Evan. "Tell her what is going on and have her meet us in Martine's room. The more hands the better." Evan followed Maggie from the room, as they headed at a near run up the stairs and to Lady Martine's bedchamber.

As they approached her door, Evan could hear his cousin crying and screaming from within the room. He also heard the old midwife shouting at Martine to be quiet.

"Damn her," spat Evan, getting to the door first. He barged into the room to find the midwife pacing back and forth while Martine lay on the bed with her knees bent and her hand on her belly. She was crying. Evan could see that the blanket was soiled with blood.

"Lady Martine!" Maggie shot into the room, putting down her basket and running to comfort the woman. "I'm here now. You're going to be fine. Please, you need not worry."

"Oh, Maggie, thank God you came! I can't have these babies without you. Gunnora doesn't know what she's doing. If you leave me to her, I know my babies and I will just die."

"Don't say that," scolded Maggie, laying her hand on Martine's belly. "Oh, your water broke," she said, seeing the wet stain on the bed. There was blood mixed in with it.

"Why didn't you help her?" Evan shouted at Gunnora.

"My lord, she's not supposed to birth her baby for another month yet," said the woman, like that made any difference. "Besides, Maggie is helping her so what does it matter?"

"Evan, she's in labor," said Maggie, with her back to Evan after checking under Martine's gown.

"Gunnora, you'll help Maggie with the birth," Evan told the old woman.

"Nay, I won't." Gunnora shook her head. "I have a nose for trouble and this has all the signs. I will not be blamed when Lady Martine and her babies die. I'm leaving." The old woman hightailed it out the door, obviously because she now knew she'd been wrong.

"I don't want to die," screamed Martine, having heard the damned midwife.

"You will not die. I promise," Maggie told her.

"Get back here," yelled Evan, starting to go after Gunnora, but Maggie stopped him.

"Nay, Evan. Let her go. Lady Martine is better off without her."

"But you need help," said Evan.

"I am sure the handmaid as well as Eleanor will be here soon."

"Ooooh! Aaaaah!" screamed Martine. "I am in so much pain! I am so scared!"

. . .

Maggie's heart about beat from her chest. She could see all the signs of distress and knew she needed to move quickly before something horrible happened.

"You'll have an easier time giving birth if you use the birthing chair instead of the bed," explained Maggie. "Plus, it will make you more accessible for me to do my job."

"I can't," cried Maggie. "I will never be able to walk over there."

"Evan," called Maggie, using his name without a title. "I need help and cannot wait for the women. It'll have to be you."

"Me?" Evan raised a brow. "Men aren't even allowed in the room when a woman is giving birth. I shouldn't even be here and you know it."

Martine cried out again.

"I need you to carry her over to the birthing chair. I'll help you. Please. We need to move quickly."

"All right," said Evan, not hesitating to do as asked when his cousin screamed in pain once more. He hurried over to the bed and gently picked up Martine. She squirmed and cried.

"I want David! I wish my husband were here," bellowed Martine.

"David is coming," Evan told her. "I sent a messenger pigeon to Blake Castle days ago telling him about your situation. I told him to come at once."

"I can't die without him at my side." Martine started bawling, cringing in pain.

"Put her down here," said Maggie, and Evan put her on

the birthing chair. There was no back to the chair and Martine was squirming so much that it seemed she'd fall off. "You'll need to sit behind her to support her during the birth," Maggie instructed, running over to the other side of the room to retrieve her basket of supplies.

"I … all right," said Evan, impressing Maggie that any man would agree to hold a woman while she gave birth. "Just don't ask me to watch because my eyes will be closed."

Maggie smiled. "You're a knight, if I must remind you. You've seen worse on the battlefield, I am sure."

"That's not what you told me before. But I suppose this will prove it."

Maggie hunkered down and positioned herself between Martine's legs and started to examine her. "Yes, the babies are trying to be born. It is time," said Maggie. "Martine, when I tell you, you'll have to push."

"I can't," cried Martine, still squirming in pain.

"Where is that handmaid with the extra towels?" Maggie glanced back at the door, wishing for more assistance. When she looked back at Martine with Evan holding her so bravely, her heart went out to both of them.

"Maggie, I am going to die, aren't I?" cried Martine. "My babies are going to be stillborns, won't they?"

"Stop it!" commanded Maggie, knowing that if she couldn't calm Martine down, this could end up being a horrible situation. It might even affect the births of the twins.

Horrible thoughts started filling Maggie's head. The day she gave birth and the death of the Lady Anora and her child haunted her still. Martine could not suffer the same ill fate. If anything happened to Martine and the twins,

Maggie would feel responsible. Maggie heard her mother's voice in her head, and the woman was telling her to stay strong. She took a deep breath and released it. "I can do this," she told herself softly. Because right now, all Lady Martine had was her, and she was counting on and believing in Maggie.

"What's the matter?" asked Evan, opening his eyes. "Is everything going to be all right?"

"Yes," she said, her hand going to the crystal pendant hanging on a cord from around her neck. She gripped it tightly. This had always been a good luck charm, so why should it be any different now? Suddenly, she realized that Martine needed the good luck more than she did. Slipping the cord over her head, Maggie removed her necklace and pressed the crystal into Martine's hands. "This is a good luck charm," she told her. "Hold it tightly and it will take away your pain and allow your babies to be born healthy. It'll also protect you."

"Maggie, is this really the time for silly superstitions?" growled Evan, trying to hold his cousin still.

"It is exactly the right time," she answered, releasing another deep breath. "These twins will be born and they will be alive and healthy, I promise you that. Lady Martine will also be fine. All she needs to do is breathe and keep holding that crystal. Can you do that, my lady?"

"Yes," said Martine, seeming to calm down a little, listening to Maggie. She clutched the crystal tightly, not letting it go. "It's working. I already feel better."

"See?" Maggie nodded at Evan and he nodded back. "It's time," she said, knowing they could not wait any longer for help to arrive. "Lady Martine, I need you to push as hard as you can. And do not stop until I tell you. These babies need your help coming into the world."

"They also need you, Maggie," said Martine. "And I know now that you are here everything will turn out for the best."

To Evan's surprise, the first baby was born quickly. It was so fast that the handmaid hadn't even returned yet with the towels.

"Oh, you have a boy," announced Maggie, just as the door opened and both the handmaid and Lady Eleanor rushed into the room.

"We're here, Martine," shouted Eleanor, running to her cousin's side. "Evan, I can hold her. You need to leave."

"Nay!" shouted Martine. "I want Evan to stay."

"Evan?" asked Maggie. "Will you?"

"I ... sure," said Evan. "I will do whatever you tell me to do, Maggie."

"Handmaid, take the baby boy and clean him up." Maggie snipped the umbilical cord and quickly tied a knot. She inspected the baby and handed him to the girl. "Be sure to wrap him in a soft blanket to keep him warm."

"Is he all right?" asked Martine, crying tears of joy now. "He is alive and well?"

"Yes. He is perfect," answered Maggie. "But we have his sibling to birth yet, so your work here is not yet done."

"I'll do it," cried Martine. "I want both my babies to live and will do whatever you say."

Evan held on to his cousin, letting her lie back against his chest for support. His knees were around the sides of her.

Martine clutched that damned crystal, and to his surprise it really seemed to help her. Or mayhap it was just the suggestion that it would, but either way the births were going smoothly so far, and he couldn't be happier. He looked the other way and not directly at her, since he wanted her to maintain her privacy in any way possible.

"Push, push!" Maggie instructed Martine as the first baby's cries filled the air from the opposite side of the room. "You need to push harder or this baby is not coming out," Maggie warned her. She looked over to Evan with a worried look on her face.

He mouthed the words, *what's wrong?*

"Handmaid, I need more hot water," said Maggie. She shook her head and examined Martine. Evan tried not to look to be polite. But when Maggie lifted her hands and he saw blood up to her elbows, he knew something was not right indeed. "More towels. Hurry," she cried.

"I've got more handmaids coming," said the girl. The door burst open and sure enough several more handmaids rushed in with towels and supplies.

"Maggie, something feels wrong," said Martine, worry tingeing her words. "Tell me. What is it?"

"Everything's fine," said Maggie in a calm voice. "The baby is breech, but I believe I can turn it around. I just need a little time. As soon as I do, I'll need you to push again."

"I don't know if I can." Evan saw Martine's face. She was spent. "I have no more energy."

Maggie worked diligently doing things that Evan believed were probably beyond her job description. He wanted to talk to her to tell her that he believed she could do it, but was afraid that he'd distract her, and that was the last thing he wanted. So instead, he continued to hold Martine, but closed his eyes. After a few minutes, he opened them again when he heard Maggie's voice.

"I did it," said Maggie, sounding pleased. "She's in position now. Lady Martine, I need you to push."

"She?" Martine cried and smiled at the same time. "It's a girl?"

"Yes," said Maggie. "But the baby is in distress and we must get her out as quickly as possible. You have to push now. Please."

"I can't." Martine looked as if she would faint.

"You can do it," Evan spoke up. "Martine, you have the damned good luck charm in your hand, so squeeze it harder and push like Maggie says," shouted Evan. "Do this for your baby. Do it for David!"

"I will," said Martine. "I will do it." She closed her eyes and bore down. Sweat dripped down the sides of her face, hitting Evan but he didn't care. He'd been in tough and uncomfortable positions before, regarding war, but this time it was all for life, not death. This time all the discomfort was for a good cause.

"I'm here, so hold on to me and use me to brace yourself as you push," Evan instructed, getting an affirmative nod from Maggie.

"Nice," he heard her say.

Evan hoped this would all be over soon, because this was more nerve-wracking than fighting the enemy on the battlefield. He wasn't sure how much longer he could be strong for Martine and for Maggie. But when he looked back at Maggie and saw how hard she was working even though she looked so tired that he wondered if she'd collapse, that gave him all the strength he needed.

"You have the best damned midwife in the nation helping you," he told his cousin. "She will make sure everything goes right. Trust in her," he said.

"I do trust Maggie. More than anyone!" exclaimed Martine, pushing again, squeezing her eyes closed and grunting as she gripped Evan's arms tightly.

The next time Evan looked over at Maggie she was smiling and holding up a baby girl still attached by the cord to Martine and covered in blood.

"You did it, Martine," said Evan. "Your daughter has been born."

"I did?" Martine opened her eyes, and cried and laughed all at the same time when she saw her baby in Maggie's hands.

"Your daughter is perfect, as well," announced Maggie, cutting the cord and handing the handmaid the baby girl. "Now we just have to make sure you birth both of the placentas so you don't get an infection."

"You don't need me for this, do you?" asked Evan, feeling queasy seeing the bloody mess and hearing all the screaming it had entailed to bring the twins into this world. He needed a strong drink of whisky, and he needed it right now.

"Am I too late?" Martine's husband David stuck his head into the room.

"David!" shouted Martine. "We have a son and a daughter both."

"Yes!" shouted David. "Can I come in?" he asked, not sure he should be there.

"Why the hell not?" said Evan. "I'm here and I could use a replacement about right now. I need a strong drink after witnessing that!"

"I told you that giving birth wasn't as easy as you thought," Maggie said with a smile.

"I know that now," said Evan.

"You can go now," Maggie told Evan wiping her cheek with the back of her hand and getting a blood smear on it. "Thank you for helping. I couldn't have done it without you."

David took Evan's place holding Martine. Evan stood up and stretched, almost retching when he looked down and saw what he supposed was what Maggie called the placentas.

"Maggie," he whispered, leaning over to talk to her while Martine and David gushed over their newborn babies. Eleanor held the baby boy and handed him to David while the handmaid handed over the little girl to Martine. "Maggie, I'd like to stay but feel like I really need to leave."

"Go," she said, looking up and smiling.

"I'd like to kiss you right now to thank you for what you've done for my cousin, but you have blood on your face."

Maggie shook her head, smiling. "I wouldn't want you to get a little blood on you. Now, go get a drink and please tell everyone about the babies. Let them know that the babies and their mother are just fine."

"I will," said Evan. "I'll check on Charles and Emma for you as well."

"Thank you," said Maggie. "I will see you later."

Evan left the room and closed the door, letting out a

deep breath. He never thought he'd ever experience anything like that. After seeing Maggie work her magic, he realized he could never let her leave. Saltwood Castle needed a good midwife like her. Because of Maggie, his cousin lived, and so did both of her babies. Maggie was a savior, and Evan wouldn't be quick to forget that.

"I love her," he mumbled to himself, knowing that no other woman could ever take the place of the amazing Maggie Whitlock.

Too damned bad he was betrothed, because he didn't want to marry anyone other than Maggie.

CHAPTER 10

"You were amazing, Maggie," Evan said from atop his horse, as they headed toward town the next morning.

Maggie's daughter was so infatuated with the new babies that she wanted to stay with Lady Martine and Lady Eleanor and help look after them. Maggie could see that Emma already had the interest, and would most likely be a midwife someday as well. Soon Maggie would start taking her to the births to get her used to seeing what happens.

"I was just doing my job," said Maggie. Her hand went to the crystal she wore and she thanked her mother silently for the lucky charm. She believed that it truly helped Martine, and that is why everything turned out so well in the end. Thankfully, Martine insisted on giving the crystal back to her, and Maggie appreciated it. After all, this was the last remembrance she had of her mother.

"Soon I will be doing my job too, and hopefully getting paid for it," said Charles, riding along with them.

Maggie's gut wrenched when he said this. She'd allowed herself to agree to let Charles work as Alan's apprentice as a locksmith for now. Something made her already regret it. "Charles, you know we most likely won't be staying in Hythe. Are you sure Alan understands that this isn't a permanent thing?"

"Why can't we stay and live in Hythe?" complained Charles. "After all, you have a permanent position as a midwife at the castle now, since that old witch left."

"Her name is Gunnora, Charles. Have a little respect. And although I've been offered the permanent position, I haven't actually accepted it yet."

"Not because of my lack of trying to convince you," mumbled Evan.

"It makes no sense why you'd say *no*," Charles continued. "After all, we will have everything we need and more than we wanted. Mayhap someday I'll be a journeyman. I'll support you then, with all the money I'll be making."

"Slow down, Brother," Maggie warned him. "You are getting ahead of yourself. We don't even know yet if you can actually do the job."

"He can," said Evan with confidence. "Alan told me that even though Charles has just started, he's been picking up the trade easily and quickly. Charles, mayhap someday I'll come spend the day at the forge with you. I have a lock I am trying to fix that has been giving me trouble. Of course, I only stop in there once a month, so it's taking a little longer than I'd like."

Maggie giggled. "At that rate, you'll have to have your grandchildren finish the job for you, because you'll be too old to see those little parts after much longer."

"I don't expect you to understand that I'm not even supposed to be at the forge since I'm a noble," Evan told her.

"Really? I heard from Lady Martine that you have a girl cousin who spends a lot of time at the forge because she married a blacksmith."

"That's my cousin Raven. She married Jonathon, but he's not really a blacksmith. He's an armorer."

"Blacksmith, locksmith, armorer, it's all the same," said Maggie with a smile.

"What? No it's not, Maggie," said Charles. "You surely know nothing about this."

"It's like saying a midwife, a healer, and an apothecary are all the same," Evan pointed out.

"Well, actually, they do kind of all overlap," stated Maggie. "I'd think now that you've assisted with a birth, you'd understand a lot more about the service I provide."

"I would if I hadn't had my eyes closed for most of it," he answered with a chuckle.

They rode up to the blacksmith's shop and stopped.

"We'll come back to get you just before it gets dark," Maggie told her brother.

"All right, but I can ride back to the castle on my own. I'm not a child." Charles made a disgruntled expression as he dismounted and tied the reins of the horse to a post.

"Until you're a little older and more used to the area, I'm going to escort you," Maggie told him.

"Don't forget to tend to the horse and keep an eye on her so she doesn't get stolen," Evan called out, as Charles hurried inside. Maggie and Evan left. They rode through town and out to the road. It was a beautiful sunny day, and this made Maggie happy.

"Don't you think you're being a little too protective of Charles?" Evan asked, after they'd ridden for a while.

"No. Not at all."

"He's not a child. He's fourteen," said Evan.

"Thirteen, actually, and I don't care what you think. I like to keep a close eye on him."

"If you don't mind me saying, you act like you're his mother."

"In a way, I am," she told him. "I watched over him many times while my mother worked and also after we lost my father. And these past four years since my mother's death have been a trying time for all of us. I made a promise to my mother and I intend to keep it."

"You never did tell me how your mother died."

"I don't like to talk about it."

"Was it something horrible?"

"Yes. Beyond horrible."

"Well, it couldn't have been the plague, since the resurge of that has come and gone long ago."

"Don't even try to guess, Evan, because I told you I don't want to talk about it."

"All right," he said with a nod. "Then how about we take a ride through the forest? I know a magical spot that I'd like to show you."

"Isn't it dangerous in the forest? There could be bandits waiting for us."

He laughed. "You are with me now, and I know how to protect a beautiful lady." He tapped the hilt of his sword to prove his point. "I assure you, we will be totally safe."

"Well, all right," she said, liking that he'd called her a lady even though she was naught but a commoner. "It does feel good to get out in the fresh air and ride again. I haven't been on a horse in a long time. I'm just glad we don't have to walk."

"Follow me," said Evan, leading the way.

Maggie didn't know where Evan was taking her, but neither did she care. She loved spending time alone with him away from the watchful eyes of others. They rode through the forest and before long ended up along the banks of a babbling brook. The sun shone down brightly upon them. Birds twittered and butterflies and dragonflies flitted around their heads.

"We're here," he announced, stopping his horse in a small clearing of tall grass.

"You're right, this place is magical," said Maggie from atop her horse, breathing in the fresh, sweet air and taking in the glorious view of nature all around her. She spotted a mother deer and her two fawns hiding in the brush. A gaggle of geese honked from the sky. Some playful squirrels chattered as they scampered across the tree branches above her head.

"May I?" he asked, suddenly standing at the side of her horse with his arms raised to assist her.

"Thank you." She let him help her down from the horse. Their bodies were touching and his hands deliciously lingered at her waist. She liked that.

"Maggie, I have a confession to make."

"What about?" She took his hand and they strolled down to the brook.

"I brought you here because I wanted to be alone with you."

"Really? Why?"

She barely got the words out before he was holding her again and kissing her. God's eyes, this felt good and she never wanted it to end.

"We can take off our shoes and walk in the water if you want."

"Nay, I don't think so," she said. "I don't like getting wet."

"Well, then how about we sit down and just watch the water?"

"I'd like that," she told him, with a peck to his cheek.

Evan spread out his cloak on the ground and they settled themselves atop it. He'd had to remove his weapon belt to sit down. After kicking off his boots he lay back with his arms behind his head.

"What are you doing?" she asked.

"I'm relaxing and enjoying the day. You should try it. Come." He patted the spot next to him. "Take off your shoes."

"Is this a ploy to get me undressed?" she asked playfully.

"Mayhap. Would it bother you if it was?"

"I don't know." She lay down next to him and kicked off her shoes. "It feels so good lying in the sun that I can't complain."

"Then don't. I know I won't." He pulled her closer and she snuggled up next to him. "I am really impressed with you, Maggie."

"It's a lot of work and a little luck, that's all."

"Nay, I don't mean your midwife skills although I have to admit that I've never seen anyone as good as you before. You honestly care about your patients."

"Of course I do," she said, reaching up and pushing a

strand of his hair from his face. "I care about you, too." She reached over and kissed him.

"Mmmm, I love your kisses." He ran his hand over the side of her face and cupped her cheek. "I was talking about how strong you are. You are not like any other woman I've ever met."

"Adversity makes one stronger, I guess. And God knows I've had more than my share of that."

"I'm so sorry to hear it."

"What about your family, Evan?" she asked, trying to change the subject before he started asking questions again about her mother that she didn't want to answer.

"What do you want to know?"

"Tell me about your parents. And your siblings."

"Well, you already know my sister, Eleanor."

"Yes. I must admit at first I thought she was a bit haughty, but the more time I spend with her, the more I realize she's truly a nice person."

"Yes, she's not bad. At times. When she stops treating me like a little brother, that is." He smiled. "She's married to Connor Wyland who used to be a noble, but then was a hangman before becoming a noble again."

"What? A hangman? You are jesting."

"Nay, I'm not. He was really an executioner. But I'll let Eleanor tell you that story since she doesn't really appreciate people talking about it."

"All right, that's fair enough," she answered. "You have another brother, don't you? I heard of him, although I haven't personally met him."

"Yes," said Evan. "Edgar, or Gar as we all call him. He is married to a merchant's daughter, Josefina. Gar is a sea captain for my father, since he loves the water and spent a lot of time on a ship as a child. Gar is really my cousin, but has been raised as my brother."

"He's your cousin? Wait. What?"

"My mother coupled with my father's brother before she married my father. That's where Gar comes from."

"She did? He does? Oh. All right."

"Mother is not the normal noblewoman, Maggie."

"What do you mean by that?"

"You see, Mother and her twin brother, my Uncle Madoc, were kidnapped as babies."

"Lady Martine's father?"

"Yes. The babies were split up and my uncle was raised as a thief, while my mother was raised as a ... a pirate."

"A pirate." Maggie smiled at him. "Now I know you are jesting. That's not funny to say things like that about your own mother, Evan."

"Maggie, I'd never lie to you," he promised, holding up his pointer finger. "She really was a pirate. Before she found out she was a noble."

"I suppose I'll have to ask your mother about that story?"

"I think it'd be a wise move. The ladies don't like talking about their past too much."

"I can see why." She giggled. "So, do you have more siblings?"

"Nay. Just a lot of cousins who all married from below the salt."

"Really?" That took her by surprise. She rather liked the idea of a noble marrying a commoner. "Is that allowed?"

"No. But my family doesn't follow rules very well."

"I guess not. Are there a lot of new babies in your family?" she asked, always curious to hear about babies because of her profession.

"The babies are starting to multiply, as you've already seen. But as for my siblings, Eleanor has a daughter named Elizabeth. Edgar, or Gar, has a son named Eliot. He and his wife adopted a stowaway named Etta."

"And your mother's name is Echo and you are Evan. Lots of E names in your family."

"Eleanor and I were named after our grandparents. But yes, E seems to be a popular letter for naming children in my family."

"I guess so. My daughter Emma is an E as well," she pointed out.

"Yes, you have an E child too," said Evan, thinking how easily Maggie would fit into his family. After all, she already had a child whose name started with E. Damn, he liked her a lot. He really enjoyed being with her. And those in his family who already met her, all liked her. She would have an easy transition being a Blackmore. But she was not. Part of him couldn't see himself marrying anyone but her, but then again, she was a commoner and he was a noble. Not to mention the fact he was already betrothed to a woman whom he didn't know or care to know.

"Maggie, I'm starting to have feelings for you," he admitted, pulling her closer as they lay on the ground, wanting to tell her exactly how he felt about her. Secretly, he was hoping to find out how she felt about him too.

"I know you do, Evan. I have feelings for you as well."

"You do? Then why don't you stay at Saltwood Castle instead of leaving?"

"Well, I don't know," she said, her smile fading. "I think it would be too hard for me to see you with another woman."

"I'm not marrying that girl my father betrothed me to, if that's what you mean."

"You're not?"

"Nay."

"I thought your father already made the alliance."

"He did. I haven't told him yet, but I will. I promise you, I will choose my own wife like the rest of my siblings and cousins. After all, why should I be any different?"

"No one should have to marry anyone they don't want to be tied down to, I guess. I believe everyone should be allowed to marry for love."

"Did you love your husband, Maggie?"

Maggie silently cursed herself for mentioning love. She supposed she accidentally led Evan to asking this question. "I barely knew George when we married," she told him. "So, no, I can't say that I loved him."

"Then why did you marry him?" Evan asked curiously.

"I thought it would help to have another person in our family. A male, that is. My mother was strong, but I saw how she struggled to raise us after my father's death. I thought I was doing the right thing."

"How old did you say you were you when your father died?"

"I was thirteen and Charles was only six."

"How long were you married?"

"I married George right after I turned sixteen. He died a few months later and that's when I discovered I was pregnant with Emma."

"So your marriage never had a chance," he said, kissing her on the nose.

"I suppose not. But I've learned to live with the hand that life dealt me."

"Then how about these hands?" he jested, slipping his hands around her and pulling her atop him, causing her to squeal.

"Evan? What are you doing?"

"Have you ever made love outside in nature?" he asked her.

"Nay. Have you?"

"Not yet, but depending on your decision, it might happen today."

Maggie felt Evan's hands closing around her bottom and giving her a slight squeeze. When she moved atop him, she felt his erection beneath her and knew exactly where this was going.

"What decision?" she asked through a breathy whisper.

"Do you want to live for the day, Maggie? Be wild and crazy?" His hands slid up her back and then around the sides of her breasts, and he gave them a light squeeze as well. She liked it. George hadn't cared about exciting her, and the one time they'd coupled was less than enjoyable for her.

"Are you asking me if I want to couple with you out here in the open where anyone might ride past and see us?"

"When you say it like that, it sounds even more exciting," said Evan with a deep chuckle.

She hit him playfully on the arm. "I don't want to put on a show for anyone."

"Then how about just for me?"

"Evan, I'm not sure this is a good idea."

"Don't worry, Maggie. We're off the beaten path and the grass is high around us. No one will see us. Just relax."

"Are you sure we'll be hidden?" she asked, looking around. They were pretty concealed, with just the open blue sky above their heads.

"I promise," he said kissing her deeply, making her head spin with delight. It felt so good to be pressed up against Evan. Their bodies already seemed to meld together even though they were still clothed.

"I always wanted to throw caution to the wind and do something crazy," she admitted. "But I never could because I always had to be the responsible one and watch after my brother and then my daughter."

"They're not here now, are they?" He waggled his eyebrows. "Want to do something crazy for the first time in your life?"

He made her laugh and Maggie liked that. She needed to laugh more in life. It felt good. Everything in her head told her not to do this, but her heart spoke louder. Her feelings for Evan won.

"I'm feeling wild and crazy if you are," she said with a giggle.

He didn't waste any time talking before pulling off her clothes and then following suit. At first she was on her back and he straddled her, kissing her on the mouth, on her chest, and her breasts. As he continued to give her pleasure, her back arched up off the ground. She felt so free. Her breathing deepened as excitement coursed through her, but she bit the side of her cheek, not wanting to cry out.

"I can see you are enjoying this but I feel you are still holding back," he told her. "Don't. Just let yourself experience every minute of our time together. Cry out if you want to. You deserve this, sweetheart."

"I love what you're doing, Evan. But you are right, I am holding back."

"Why?"

"Because, I am so ready for this that I feel as if I am going to burst. Please, I need you inside me right now."

"As you wish. But first, you need to be on top." He wrapped his arms around her and rolled to his back, pulling her atop him.

"Are you sure about this?" she asked.

"More than sure, sweetheart. I am a heavy weight upon you and this way you can move freely and enjoy it more."

"Then you'll have to guide me with what to do. It's been such a long time and I never really knew what I was doing the first time."

"There are no rules when it comes to making love," he told her. "We can do whatever we want."

"So, I don't have to worry about doing it wrong?"

"You couldn't do anything wrong if you tried, Maggie. You are perfect."

Evan's confidence in her made her even more excited to be with him, naked out in nature. She had never done anything like this before, and it was refreshing, new, and adventurous. Suddenly, all her fears were washed away, and she felt no obligations or worries. Right now, she was happier than she'd ever been in her entire life.

Being with Evan felt good. It felt right. She was quickly losing her heart to him. She needed to know how it felt to make love with him, and now it was actually going to happen.

He readied her with his hand even though she was more than prepared. Then, while lying beneath her, he took her hips in his hands and positioned her right over his hardened manhood.

"I'll go slow," he told her. "Just to make sure you can take in all of me."

Gently, he slipped inside her just a little and she gasped.

"Did I hurt you?" He stopped, and that wasn't at all what she wanted.

"Believe me, you didn't hurt me. That was a gasp because I cannot believe how good it feels."

"Then I should continue?"

"Oh, never mind. I'll do it myself," she told him impatiently, lowering herself over him, letting his tool of love fill her completely.

"I like a feisty woman who knows what she wants," he told her. Then, using his hands to help her move her hips, he moved his hips to meet her. They did the dance of love, each one of his thrusts becoming stronger as he grew closer and closer to his release.

Maggie didn't mind. She liked the feeling and the freedom. Before she knew it, he'd hit a spot that sent her spiraling out of control with pure pleasure.

"Ooooh, aaaah, this feels so good," she said, as they moved faster and faster, their bare bodies slapping together, with thankfully no one there to hear them.

"Maggie, you are perfect and I hope you never leave me,"

he whispered, his words causing her to lose control. She didn't hide her sounds of ecstasy as she reached her peak and found completion. With her eyes closed, she swore she saw bright stars in hues of purple and pink behind her shut lids.

"Oh, Evan, I never want to leave you," she admitted, seeming to cause him to become even more excited, even though she didn't think it was possible.

He made sounds like a bear, and it wasn't hard to figure out just when he'd found his release and spilled his seed within her. The crazy thought that they might have just made a baby caused her to climax once more.

Finally, things calmed down and she rolled off of him, settling under his arm while laying her cheek against his chest.

"God's eyes, that was wonderful," he finally said, stroking her hair gently with his free hand.

"I agree," she said, kissing his chest. Without meaning to, she fell asleep next to him. And when she awoke, he was still in the same position, holding her, protecting her, making her feel safe and in no hurry to leave.

She didn't think they'd been at the brook that long, but when she noticed the sun getting lower in the sky, she realized nightfall was already moving in.

"Oh, we'd better get up and get dressed," she said, sitting up.

"What's your hurry?" He looked at her with those sexy green eyes. Just by his stare she found herself getting hot again. "If you're cold I can warm you up."

"Oh, believe me, I'm not cold," she told him, kissing him quickly on the lips. "It is just that we need to ride back to town to get Charles, and it will take a while. I don't want to be traveling on the road at night if we don't have to."

"I understand your concern," he said, sitting up as they both started to dress. "Although, you need to understand that I am more than capable of protecting you as well as Charles in the dark."

"I know you are. Thank you," she said, giving him one last kiss before donning her shoes. "I have never felt safer than I do with you, Evan. I don't know what I'm going to do without you."

"You don't have to be without me," he told her, standing up to strap on his weapon belt. "I want you to stay at Saltwood Castle, Maggie. Forever."

Maggie's heart skipped a beat as she looked down to tie her bodice. Evan was asking her to stay, but she was afraid to ask him exactly what he meant by that. She figured he wanted her to live at Saltwood Castle, but probably just as the midwife. Right now she wanted so much more. He had said he wanted to be with her forever, but what was missing were the words *I want to marry you, Maggie.*

Her heart ached, because she couldn't stay at the castle and watch him marry someone else. It would hurt too deeply. She'd rather be back on the road searching for work than to live comfortably with him but never have him as her husband.

"What do you say, Maggie? Will you stay with me permanently?"

"I—I don't know." She wanted to ask him what that would involve, but being too scared to do so, she stayed silent. If he'd meant to keep her around just as a midwife and for a possible tryst, she'd be heartbroken. Mayhap, she decided, it was better that she didn't know. "I'll have to think about it," she answered sadly. "We'd better hurry because Charles will be waiting. I don't want him doing anything crazy, like leaving without us and riding home alone."

"Nay. We wouldn't want anyone doing anything crazy now, would we?" He sounded sad when he said it, even though they had both just done something very crazy and she didn't regret it at all. He probably sounded this way because she didn't give him the answer he wanted. Still, she was being guarded, because she'd known too much sorrow in her life. She couldn't agree to staying forever at Saltwood Castle without a stronger commitment from him that involved more than just being his mistress. Sadly, she was afraid that was all she'd ever be.

She knew Evan was betrothed, even though he also said he wouldn't really marry the girl. Still, Maggie wasn't sure she believed him. How could he, a noble, get out of a betrothal for the purpose of an alliance without causing a battle between his family and the other for breaking the agreement? It would only bring trouble, and she didn't want trouble for anyone. Especially not for Evan.

When they were making love, she swore he purposely said things to her that made her think he wanted to marry her, even though he was vague about his meaning. Could he have done this just to trick her into saying she'd stay? After all, from her experiences, nobles only thought about themselves and were far from honest. But Evan wasn't like that.

Was he?

If so, he certainly had her fooled. This doubt she had

bothered her more right now than even making love out in the open.

She mounted her horse, not feeling like talking, just wanting to get back to the castle and to her daughter. To her warm blankets and pallet. To sleep and rest and think. Today she'd been crazy and carefree. As good as it felt, she had the awful feeling in her gut that she was going to pay for this happiness, eventually. A fear crept in that it was all about to be taken away from her, and that she decided, was even worse than being crazy.

CHAPTER 11

Over a week had passed since they'd made love, and it bothered Evan that Maggie still hadn't given him an answer. He wanted to be with her, but somehow it didn't seem as if she wanted to be with him.

Evan pushed the food back and forth atop his trencher, confused and frustrated by this situation. Ever since they'd made love, it seemed as if Maggie had been doing her best to avoid him. She'd been spending most of her time up in the ladies' solar with Eleanor and Martine. He'd heard that she even offered to watch Martine's newborn twins because she loved the babies so much. The women even ate meals in Martine's chamber instead of joining the men in the great hall, keeping to themselves and making Evan feel totally ignored.

"Evan, if you're not going to eat that duck, I'll take it," said Daegel from next to him atop the dais.

"What?" He looked up and saw Daegel's eyes devouring his share of the food. "Sure, take it. I'm not hungry." He slid his trencher over to his cousin. Then he looked below the salt once more, hoping to spot Maggie but she wasn't there and neither was little Emma. Charles was there though, never one to miss a meal. He'd been getting along wonderfully with the servants and other boys his age. His confidence had seemed to grow lately since he'd been spending so much time in town with Alan as the man's new apprentice. The boy couldn't stop talking about his job, and showing locks and keys he'd brought home to all of his new friends.

"Where's Maggie?" asked Daegel, using his spoon to scrape all of Evan's food onto his own trencher. "I haven't seen much of her lately."

"Neither have I," he answered with a sigh.

"What's the matter? Did you two have a spat?" Daegel took a big bite of food and then picked up his cup to drink.

"Nay. Just the opposite, actually. We made love out by the brook."

Daegel spit a stream of wine through the air. "You did what?"

"You heard me." Evan picked up his goblet to drink.

"Well, Cousin, you must not have been any good at bedding her, since she won't talk to you anymore."

"Shut up," snarled Evan. "You don't know what you say. We are both mad about each other."

"Mmmm hmmm." Daegel wiped his mouth with the back of his hand and took another drink. "So, did you tell her this?"

"I did. And she returned the feelings."

"And?" Daegel's thick brows arched.

"And what?" Evan raised his palms in the air in surrender.

"Did you say ... anything else to her regarding the way you feel?"

"Yes. I asked her to stay at Saltwood Castle with me. Forever. But she still hasn't given me her answer and it is driving me mad. I don't know what to do." Evan took another drink of wine.

"That's odd. You told the commoner you want to marry her, and she has yet to give you her answer?"

Now it was Evan's turn to spit a stream of wine through the air. "Marry her?" he asked. "Who said anything about that? Nay, of course I didn't ask her to marry me. Why would I?"

"Well, if you two are crazy about each other, it seems the next step would be marriage."

Evan felt in his heart that Maggie was truly the one he wanted to make his wife, but something inside made him hesitate to ask her. He wasn't sure if it stemmed from the fact that he still wasn't sure she had feelings for him like he did for her, or if it was something entirely different. Like already being betrothed.

"Daegel, if I must remind you, I'm betrothed and supposed to be marrying a noblewoman. That creates a little problem."

"Oh. So you're going to stick with that as your excuse?"

"What does that mean?" Evan saw a kitchen maid carrying a tray of sweets and he waved her over. "Leave the tray," he told the girl, picking up a hand tart and taking a bite. Mayhap he could drown his sorrows eating baked goods, which were his favorite thing to eat.

"Consider this," said Daegel. "Mayhap the reason she didn't answer yet is because she is waiting for you to actually come out and ask her to marry you."

"I can't do that. Not until I break off my betrothal first. You know that." Evan downed the tart and picked up a piece of seed cake next, taking a big bite.

"Do you really intend to break off the agreement of your betrothal before your father returns?"

"I'll have to, I guess," said Evan with a shrug, taking another swig of wine. "Father said my betrothed will arrive with her father before he returns, so I will have to handle it. Actually, I'm surprised they haven't arrived by now."

"You really plan on telling your betrothed to her face that you won't marry her?"

"Yes. That is what I really intend to do." He picked up his goblet for another drink.

"Sir Evan," said his uncle, Brother Ruford, standing at the front of the table from the floor, looking up at them. "I have someone I would like you to meet."

"Not now, Brother Ruford," griped Evan, wanting to be left alone to think.

"I'm afraid this can't wait, my lord." The monk moved closer to the dais and leaned in to speak. "You see, your betrothed and her father have arrived, and they are waiting to meet you out in the courtyard."

Needless to say, once again, Evan involuntarily spit wine through the air.

～

"It's been so long already and you still haven't named your twins?" asked Maggie, holding her daughter on her lap while Emma held the newborn baby girl. That was hard for Maggie to comprehend, since she'd been thinking of names for her children someday ever since she was a child.

They were in Lady Martine's bedchamber, along with the nursemaid and Lady Eleanor. Today, Eleanor had her six-month-old daughter, Elizabeth, in the room with them. Elizabeth was on her lap with her doll. The little girl squirmed, seeming to want to be put down. Lady Martine was in a chair holding her new son.

"Nay, that's not true. We've finally decided," said Martine. "Since David had to go back to Steepleton this morning to tend to the tavern, we agreed on a decision before he left."

"Well? What are their names?" asked Maggie. "I cannot wait to hear them."

Martine coddled the little boy, making baby sounds to him. "We decided that each of our babies are going to be named after one of our parents. We used his mother's name. Our daughter is Greta, since I didn't like the name Elrod, which was the name of David's father."

"Oh, I like the name, Greta," said Maggie, smiling at the baby on her lap. "Hello, cute little Greta."

"Greta is my baby," said Emma, possessively hugging the child to her.

"Eleanor and Martine laughed.

"No, Emma, she is not yours. Her mama is Lady Martine," Maggie reminded her. "What did you name your son, Lady Martine?"

"Well, since we needed a boy's name and my father's name is Madoc and David didn't want to name our son that, we decided to look to other family members instead."

"She couldn't name him after our grandfather, since Evan is already named after him," spoke up Lady Eleanor.

"Are you sure you don't want to call him Elrod?" asked Maggie. "After all, that is an E name, and this family seems to have lots of those."

"Nay, I think I'll save that E name for when Eleanor has a son," said Martine with a smile. "After all, it is her family that has all the E's, not mine. We named our son William, after my father's brother."

"William. Such a noble name," said Maggie. "I love it."

"Me too," agreed Eleanor. "But I want to tell you, Martine, that you might get your wish faster than you think regarding me taking that E name for my child." Eleanor smiled, mischief dancing in her eyes.

"Eleanor, I'm confused," answered Martine. "I have no idea what you are talking about."

"Oh, I know what that means," Maggie said, feeling excited for the woman. "You are pregnant again, aren't you, Lady Eleanor?"

"Yes. I think so." Eleanor blushed, giving her daughter a squeeze. "Little Elizabeth might be having a brother or sister soon."

"I knew it!" said Maggie. "I could tell by your glow lately."

"Really?" Eleanor made a silly face. "I don't even know for sure yet if I am truly with child, but I have missed my courses two months in a row, so I am guessing it to be true. I haven't told Connor yet. I wanted to be sure first."

"Oh, Eleanor, congratulations." Martine was thrilled, the same as Maggie. "You have to promise me you'll make Maggie your midwife. She is wonderful and you shouldn't go with anyone else."

"Well, I suppose I will if Maggie plans on staying here at Saltwood Castle."

"Are you staying?" asked Martine. "Please say yes. We need you."

"I'm not sure yet," said Maggie, looking down at Emma and the baby. "Sir Evan has asked me to stay on for good, but I haven't given him an answer yet."

"Why not?" asked Martine, blinking in confusion.

"Emma, do you want to play with Elizabeth?" asked Maggie, not wanting to discuss this with her daughter listening.

"I'll take the baby." The nursemaid walked over and scooped up little Greta.

"Yes. I want to play with Elizabeth's doll." Emma didn't have a doll of her own. Since they moved so often and Maggie always had so much on her mind, she'd completely neglected the little girl's needs. Maggie realized now that she should have gotten her daughter a doll long ago. Emma loved babies and loved pretending she had her own. Yes, she needed to get Emma a doll soon.

"Elizabeth is young yet, so you need to be gentle with her, Emma," Maggie reminded the little girl, putting her down on the floor.

"Come on, Elizabeth." Emma ran over and held out her arms. Eleanor put her daughter and the doll on the floor. Elizabeth, not yet able to walk, crawled toward her. The children played, not paying any attention to the adults.

"Now, tell us the real reason why you didn't take up Evan on his offer," said Martine, obviously knowing too well that Maggie wasn't telling them everything.

"Yes," said Eleanor, moving closer to talk with the women. "Did he do something . . . inappropriate with you? My brother can tend to be a real cur sometimes."

"Well ... I suppose most people would think making love in the outdoors is inappropriate, but I rather liked it," Maggie answered with a wide smile.

Eleanor's jaw dropped but Martine squealed.

"Oh, Maggie, I think you might be joining our family soon," said Martine. "Don't you, Eleanor?"

"Well, as much as I'd like Maggie to be part of our family, you are forgetting that Evan is betrothed to a noblewoman who should be arriving here any day now," Eleanor pointed out.

"I didn't forget." Maggie stood up, suddenly feeling very hot. "That is why I didn't answer him. I don't think I'll be able to accept seeing Evan with another woman. Would you mind if I opened the window? I am very warm."

"Go ahead," said Martine. "So, Evan didn't ask you to marry him? Really?"

"Nay," said Maggie, walking over to the window. "He told me he wasn't going to marry his betrothed, but he never mentioned wanting me to be his wife instead."

"Oh, don't worry," said Eleanor. "I'm sure it will all work out. After all, his betrothed isn't here yet, so mayhap the girl's father has changed his mind about letting her marry Evan. She will probably never even show up."

Maggie pulled open the shutter and peered down into

the courtyard. Evan and Daegel were with Brother Ruford, and they were greeting a man and a woman who had just arrived in a wagon pulled by a horse. "I think you're wrong, Eleanor, because it looks to me like they have just arrived."

"Oh, no!" Martine got up and hurried over to the window.

"I wonder who she is?" asked Eleanor. "Father left in such a hurry that he never told us." She got up to join them as well.

"Doesn't Evan know who he's marrying?" asked Martine.

"I don't think so," said Maggie. "He didn't seem to even know her name."

"Eleanor, didn't your father say that Brother Ruford had all the information?" Martine peered out the window.

"Yes." Eleanor looked out as well. "But Evan probably never even asked our uncle about it, knowing him. My brother tends to wait until the last minute, or at least until he is forced to do something, before he actually goes ahead and does it."

Maggie was curious and stretched her neck to see if the girl was pretty or not, but the girl's back was toward them. Evan took his betrothed's hand and kissed it, which bothered Maggie immensely. She heard the girl laugh, and something about the sound of her voice made Maggie sick to her stomach, but she didn't know why. She had an odd feeling that the girl and her father seemed familiar, but without actually seeing their faces she had no reason to feel this way.

"I can't see her face," said Martine.

"Well, mayhap we should go down there and welcome

them then," suggested Eleanor. "We'll get a good look that way."

"Oh, yes, I agree," said Martine, as the two noblewomen started for the door. "Are you coming, too, Maggie?"

"Oh, I'm not sure that would be proper." As curious as Maggie was about Evan's betrothed, she realized she was a commoner and had no right being around the nobles.

"Hell with proper, you will join us," said Eleanor, waving her hand carelessly through the air. This surprised Maggie and almost made her laugh. She was starting to like Eleanor more and more every day. "I know you are just as curious as to whom Evan is marrying as we are, so let's go."

"I agree," said Martine. "You are coming with us and we won't hear another word about it."

"Well, I suppose it wouldn't hurt." Maggie headed for the door.

"Mama, I want to come with you." Emma ran over, and Maggie scooped her up into her arms.

"I'll watch Elizabeth and put the twins down for a nap," the nursemaid called out to them as they left the room.

"I want to ride with Sir Evan on his horse again," whined Emma. "I like him. Can he be my father?"

Maggie found herself dumbstruck, realizing now that even though the little girl had been playing, she had also been listening to their entire conversation. "Emma, it would be best if you didn't ask questions like that," scolded Maggie.

"Why not?" asked the little girl. "Is it because Sir Evan is going to marry someone else? I wish he would marry you, Mama."

"So do I," Maggie mumbled to herself, kissing her daughter on her head. She followed Eleanor and Martine down the corridor and out to the courtyard, the knot in her stomach twisting harder, making her feel as if she should have stayed back in the bedchamber, after all.

CHAPTER 12

"Sir Evan, I'd like you to meet your betrothed, Lady Beatrice Bohun ,and her father, Lord Florian of Ashenden," Brother Ruford announced, standing in the courtyard to introduce him to their guests.

"Welcome, Lady and Lord Ashenden," said Evan, his heart not at all in greeting his betrothed and her father. He kissed the back of the girl's hand as was proper, feeling as if he were cheating on Maggie for some reason. Brother Ruford stood with them, watching over everything in Evan's father's absence. "I'd like you to meet my cousin, Sir Daegel Blake," said Evan, and Daegel stepped forward.

"Charmed," said the woman, letting Daegel kiss her hand, but Evan swore the girl cringed. She was dressed in the gown of a noble, but wore an ugly green cloak like her father. The color reminded Evan of the murky waters of the moat.

"Lord Ashenden is here with the papers to sign to seal the betrothal and finalize the alliance," Ruford explained.

"Yes, that's right," said Lord Florian, seeming impatient and agitated just being here. "I should be at the king's funeral, but had to come here. Let's get this over with quickly so I can be on my way."

"I suppose we could go to the solar and sign the papers," said Ruford.

Evan had to stall this until he could think of a way to get out of marrying the girl. She wasn't ugly, but seemed awfully stiff and stuffy. She hadn't stopped looking down her nose at him since she got here. Thankfully, he saw his sister and cousin coming across the courtyard.

"Oh, I'd like to introduce you to some of my family," said Evan, waving the girls over.

"That's not necessary." Lord Ashenden scowled.

"If we're going to be family soon, I am sure you'll want to meet them," said Evan.

"We'll be living in Ashenden, so we'll have no need to ever see them," said Beatrice with a sniff.

"Living in Ashenden?" Evan looked over at Ruford and the monk shrugged. Evan was sure his father would never have agreed to that! He'd have to look over the papers closely to make sure these people weren't trying to deceive him.

"Hello," called out Eleanor, as the girls approached them.

"This is my sister, Lady Eleanor Wyland and my cousin, Lady Martine Stone," said Evan, taking their hands and bringing them forward. "Ladies, this is Lady Beatrice Bohun and her father, Lord Florian. They are from Ashenden." The girls curtsied and greeted the newcomers. Then there was an awkward silence that fell over them. Evan knew he had to say something. "I've never been to Ashenden, nor do I know anything about it, but for some reason it seems so familiar to me."

"Ashenden is where Maggie comes from, isn't it?" asked Martine.

Hearing her say Maggie's name made him remember. Evan turned to his cousin. She was right. That's why it seemed familiar. "Yes, I think so."

"Who is Maggie?" asked Lord Florian.

"She is our midwife here at the castle. Mayhap you know her," said Evan. "I'll have to introduce you to her."

"She was right behind us," said Eleanor, looking over her shoulder. "Oh, here she comes now. You can ask her yourself if she knows them."

Maggie cranked the bucket from the well up to the top, having to fetch little Elizabeth's doll out of the water after Emma had tossed into the well as they walked by. Maggie had been so distracted knowing that Evan's betrothed had arrived that she hadn't even noticed that Emma still had the doll on her when they left the keep.

"Emma, that is not nice to throw Elizabeth's toy into the well. She's probably crying and looking for it right now. Why did you do that?"

Maggie tried to wring the water out of the doll that was constructed mainly from cloth and stuffed with straw. Little Emma stood at the foot of the well pouting.

"I wanted Sir Evan to get it for me," said Emma, stubbornly crossing her arms over her chest.

"Sweetheart, Sir Evan is a knight. He has better things to

do than to be fishing in the water for soggy dolls. Now, don't do that again."

She gave the doll to Emma and picked her up, looking across the courtyard for Martine and Eleanor. It was hard to see past all the people bustling to and fro, but she spotted Martine waving her over.

"We are going to meet some people, and I want you to be on your best behavior. Do you understand?"

"Yes, Mother," said the little girl, her arms hugging Maggie around her neck as they walked. The soggy doll was dangling from Emma's hand.

"Maggie, we want you to meet someone who you might already know," called out Martine as Maggie walked up to the group, stopping right behind Evan. He moved to the side and Maggie got a full view of his betrothed as well as her father. She hadn't expected this and these were the last people she ever wanted to see.

"Beatrice!" she gasped, almost dropping Emma since she was so shocked to see the girl.

"Maggie?" Beatrice's eyes opened in surprise.

"Oh, it seems you two already know each other," said Evan, having no idea what happened between Maggie and Beatrice years ago. "Were you two friends when Maggie lived in Ashenden?" Evan asked innocently.

Maggie wanted to curl up and die right now. She couldn't bring herself to say a word. Her heart beat so quickly that the blood rushing through her body almost deafened her ears. This was the daughter of the noblewoman who had died the day Maggie gave birth to Emma. It was also the girl and her father who were responsible for executing her mother!

"Far from friends," sneered Beatrice.

Maggie didn't respond.

"Sir Evan, Elizabeth's dolly fell in the well and almost drowned," said Emma, holding up the wet doll to show him. "I wanted you to save her, but Mother said you didn't have time to help me."

"Oh, I'm sorry to hear about the doll," said Evan, smiling at the little girl. "I am sure she'll be fine and probably just wanted a bath."

Maggie's heart went out to Evan for taking a moment to try to comfort her daughter. Still, she couldn't help but notice the disapproving glares he was getting from Lord and Lady Ashenden for even talking to a commoner.

"Hold me," begged Emma, reaching out for him. Before Maggie could stop the child, she was basically crawling out of Maggie's arms and trying to get to Evan.

"Careful there, sweetheart, before you fall," said Evan. His arms shot out and he scooped up Emma, taking the little girl from Maggie without hesitation. He held Emma against him with one strong arm. Emma smiled.

"Blackmore, we have business to attend to," complained Lord Ashenden.

"Yes," agreed Beatrice. "And I do not approve of my betrothed taking such an interest in commoners, let alone spend time talking with them. Especially when other nobles are present."

Before Evan could respond to their snide remarks, Emma shouted out something to them that Maggie had rather wished she hadn't.

"My mama loves Sir Evan and he's going to be my father

soon," Emma blurted out, making Maggie feel as if she were about to faint.

"What's this?" asked Beatrice.

"Blackmore, what kind of a sick man are you?" growled Lord Florian.

"Pardon me?" asked Evan. It was clear that he had no idea what was going on, or why Emma had even said that.

"Is that *her* child?" asked Beatrice with a sniff, once again throwing her nose in the air.

"Yes, this is Maggie's daughter, Emma. She's four," said Evan. "So, did you know Maggie when her mother was a midwife working in Ashenden?"

"Oh, we knew her all right," said Beatrice, contempt dripping from every word.

"That's nice," said Evan, still having no idea what had transpired.

"Nice?" bellowed Lord Ashenden. "How can you say such a thing?"

"What do you mean?" asked Evan.

Beatrice spoke up next, spilling the rest of Maggie's secrets. "It is not nice, Sir Evan. After all, it was her mother's fault that my mother and baby brother died!"

"Pardon me? What did you say?" Evan's smile dissipated when he realized that mayhap Maggie and the Ashendens were not friends after all, but perhaps enemies.

"That's right," said Lord Florian. "Her mother chose to help Maggie give birth to that whelp you're holding instead of helping a noblewoman, which should have been her only priority."

"I'm confused." Evan looked over at Maggie who seemed as pale as a ghost. "Maggie, what are they talking about?"

"I know them, Sir Evan," Maggie finally answered with a sigh. "I know them and I am sorry to say that I despise them too." Maggie had such anger in her eyes that Evan didn't even know her anymore.

"Did something happen between you?" asked Martine.

"You are damned right it did," said Beatrice, looking like she was ready to bite off Maggie's head. "Her mother saved her own grandchild instead of my baby brother. Because of it, my brother was a stillborn. To make matters even worse, my mother died that day too, all because of Maggie and her mother."

"Nay," said Evan, shaking his head, not wanting to believe this. "You must be mistaken, Lady Ashenden. Maggie's mother was the best midwife in the land. She never lost a baby or even a mother the entire time. Maggie told me so."

"Well, she lies," said Lord Florian with a grunt. "That girl's daughter does not deserve to live."

Emma whimpered and hid her face against Evan's chest.

"Now, wait a minute," said Evan, pulling the girl closer and rubbing a comforting hand over her back. "I will not tolerate this kind of talk in my courtyard. Especially not about my midwife and this young, innocent girl." He nodded at Emma in his arms.

"Why not?" asked Beatrice. "After all, every word of it is true. Maggie and her mother were responsible for my mother's death as well as the death of my brother. Now, Maggie and her daughter need to die as well!" screamed Beatrice, scaring Emma and making her cry.

"Stop it!" yelled Maggie, taking Emma back from Evan. "You are horrible people and I want nothing to do with you ever again. Leave me and my family alone."

"Maggie, I've been looking for you." Charles walked up, and Maggie reached out and pulled him to her to protect him as well. "What's going on?" asked Charles.

"Charles, we're leaving at once. Let's get out of here." Maggie turned and nearly ran with Charles and Emma, making her way to the castle.

"Cousin?" Daegel walked over and talked in a soft voice. "What the hell is going on here? It's not what I expected at all. You seem to have angered two women."

"I wish I knew," said Evan. "And I didn't anger any of them. This is a feud that seems to have been going on for quite some time now. Stay here and talk to the Ashendens. I need to go after Maggie."

"Me? Nay, don't do this to me, Evan. It's not fair," muttered Daegel.

"I want that woman to be executed," ordered the pompous Beatrice. "Father, do something about it. Make it happen."

"Yes, Blackmore, my daughter is right," said Lord Ashenden. "That girl is responsible for the deaths of my wife and child. I demand she is imprisoned at once and condemned to death."

"Nay!" shouted Evan. "No one is going to touch Maggie or her family. And you will not tell me what to do in my own household," snapped Evan.

"But that girl and her mother are murderers," said Lord Florian. "You cannot let them get away with killing nobles."

"I am sorry that your wife and son died," Evan told him.

"But I am sure Maggie's mother did everything she could to save them. It is no one's fault."

Martine, Daegel, and Eleanor huddled together, watching but not saying a word.

"Now, now, everyone please calm down." Ruford tried to intervene to make peace between them.

"Father, I don't want to marry this man anymore," Beatrice retorted. "He is siding with the enemy. Besides, I think he's already coupled with Maggie. I won't have a husband who has been bedding a murdering commoner."

"I'm sure there's a misunderstanding," said Ruford, as Evan became madder and madder. "Sir Evan, tell your betrothed that you didn't touch the midwife in that way."

"Why would I say that when it isn't even true?" snarled Evan.

"What?" Beatrice's eyes widened. "So you did bed her! Even though we were betrothed."

"That's right," said Evan. "I not only made love to Maggie, but we did it in the forest right out in the open."

"Evan, stop it," warned Eleanor, but Evan was so angry that he kept on going.

"Lady Beatrice, I wouldn't marry you if you were the last living wench in the world," he continued. "You are pretentious, a liar, and a downright wretched bitch."

"Oh, crap. This can't end well," he heard Daegel mutter.

"I am in love with Maggie," Evan told them, liking the way it sounded as he said it aloud. "Maggie is kind, selfless, sweet, and caring about others, never thinking about herself. She is strong and protective of her family, and skilled in healing and birthing babies. Maggie is beautiful and has a heart of gold. She has all the qualities I am looking for in a wife. I love her, and I more than intend to marry her instead of someone like you!"

"Brother Ruford, this is preposterous!" shouted Lord Florian. "I will have a word with the Lord Warden when he returns, because I won't let my daughter marry his outspoken, troublesome son!"

"Please, can we just go inside and have a drink and talk this over?" asked Ruford in his quiet manner. His face became redder than a beet.

"Nay, let them leave," said Eleanor, stepping forward. "And do not threaten us again, because it'll only get you imprisoned. You are talking to the children of the Lord Warden of the Cinque Ports. If you're not careful, you'll be taking the hangman's place just to save your life."

"Lady Eleanor, please go back to the castle with Lady Martine." Brother Ruford tried to guide them with a gentle push.

"I agree with my cousins," said Daegel next, his hand on the hilt of his sword. "I wouldn't anger us, if I were you. I am a knight and so is Sir Evan, and I warn you, we know how to use our weapons to protect our people."

"Daegel, Evan, this has got to stop," said Ruford, seeming so flustered that Evan wasn't sure he wasn't going to drop dead.

"Leave here and never return." Evan rested his hand on the hilt of his sword as a subliminal warning.

"This is going to end in battle, I warn you," said Lord Florian, pulling his daughter to him. "We had an alliance and you are breaking it."

"May I see the papers that are to be signed for the betrothal?" asked Ruford, holding out his hand.

"It is all right here in writing." Lord Ashenden pulled out the contract and handed it to Ruford. "As you see, we have an agreement with the Lord Warden that cannot be broken."

Ruford flipped through the papers and shook his head. "What I see is a contract that is yet to be signed by both parties," said the monk. "Therefore, I believe this betrothal is not valid." Ruford tore up the marriage agreement and let the pieces of paper flutter to the ground.

"You will be sorry you did that, you blasted monk!" screamed Ashenden.

"Refrain from speaking to a holy man in such a manner," Evan warned him, wanting to shout with joy that his uncle just tore up the contract. "I believe it would be wise for you two to leave Saltwood Castle now and never return."

"Come, Beatrice, we're leaving. But you have not heard the end of this," screamed the man, as he helped his daughter get into the wagon. The driver turned the wagon and they headed out the gate.

"Thank you for that, Ruford," Evan told his uncle.

"I couldn't let you marry her," said the monk.

"But can you really tear up the contract like that?" asked Martine.

"It was yet to be signed, so there wasn't yet a finalized betrothal," the monk explained. "I purposely tore up the papers so those two conniving, no-good people could not try to forge the signatures."

"Father isn't going to like hearing about this," said Eleanor.

"I'll fill him in on everything that happened," said Ruford. "The Lord Warden will understand, and I am sure he will agree with my actions."

"Make sure they really leave and don't try to return," said Evan, turning to go.

"Wait. Where are you going?" asked Daegel.

"I need to find Maggie, because she has a lot of explaining to do."

CHAPTER 13

Maggie couldn't even see through her tears as she hurriedly packed her things, not able to believe what just happened in the courtyard. Now she wished she had never gone out there at all.

"Who were those people, Maggie?" asked Charles, sitting down on the pallet in the small room that they shared, while Emma lay on the floor crying.

"They are the people who executed our mother." Maggie had never told Charles what really happened to their mother. He'd asked about her through the years, and Maggie had told him that their mother was sick and died in Ashenden. Now, she wished she had told him the truth long ago.

"Mother was executed?" Charles's head snapped up and he frowned. "Why?"

"Emma, stop crying," Maggie told her daughter, who lay face down on the floor, hugging the soggy doll. "The night Emma was born, Mother was also helping to birth Lady

Ashenden's baby. But there were complications, and the noblewoman and her baby died that day. The woman you saw in the courtyard is the daughter of the dead noble. She is also the one who blamed me and Mother for the deaths, even though it wasn't our fault." Maggie shoved more clothes into a bag, and yanked close the drawstrings. "Charles, I need your help packing our things. If we don't get out of here, we will be executed next. These nobles will never stop blaming us, and neither will they ever stop trying to track us down."

"I don't want to leave here, Maggie. I like my job and I have friends for the first time in my life." Charles did nothing to help.

"I want Sir Evan," wailed Emma, only making Maggie feel even worse.

Maggie had never told any of this to Evan even though he'd tried to get her to talk about her mother. Now she wished she would have also told him what happened, because he was going to think the worst of her. It was rotten luck that his betrothed just happened to be the girl whom Maggie hated and feared more than anyone in the world.

Out of habit, her hand went to her crystal to calm her, but she couldn't feel it. She grabbed at her clothing and then her hand went to her neck, as she realized that her good luck charm was gone. "My crystal! It's missing. Where is it?" She looked around but couldn't find it anywhere. She hadn't even noticed that she'd lost it until now.

"Maggie," called out Evan from the other side of the door. He knocked, but she did nothing to open it. Charles jumped up and pulled open the door.

"Sir Evan!" Emma saw him and ran to him, hugging him around his knees. She continued to cry.

"Why are you crying, sweetheart?" he asked, picking up Emma and reaching out to smooth down her hair. Maggie still clutched the wet doll.

"My mama is going to die!" shouted Emma. "I don't want her to die. Please save her, Sir Evan. Please help her."

"No one is going to die," he told the little girl. "I promise I won't let that happen."

Maggie picked up the bags and looked over at her brother. "Let's go, Charles. Get Emma. We need to start walking."

"You're not going anywhere," Evan told her. "You are all staying right here."

"Why would you even want me to stay after what Lady Beatrice and her father told you? You heard them say that my mother and I are responsible for the deaths of Lady Anora and her baby."

"Are you?" he asked quietly.

"Does it really matter what I say at this point? You are a noble, and will side with other nobles instead of commoners, I'm sure."

"Maggie, where is this coming from?" asked Evan. "I think we need to talk. You should have told me about all this before instead of keeping it from me. It makes you seem ... guilty."

"If you believe I am guilty, then there is no reason for me to even stay here any longer, trying to convince you that I'm not." She shoved the bags at Charles and took Emma from him. "Please step aside, because we are leaving."

•   •   •

"Maggie, stop it," said Evan, as she pushed past him and Charles followed. "I am sure this is all just a misunderstanding."

"They'll never stop coming for me and my family. We will be executed, just like they did to my mother. I cannot and will not let that happen." She continued to walk and Evan followed.

"Maggie, nay, I won't let you leave."

"You're marrying Beatrice now," she said, as he followed her through the kitchen.

"I'm not. I broke off the betrothal."

"Then you'll go to battle with them for breaking the alliance. Once again, I am sure I will somehow be blamed."

"Don't leave," he begged, but she kept on walking. "Maggie, I love you," he blurted out, and all the servants heard him. They stopped working and watched and listened.

"Evan, but we both know this can't work, no matter how we feel about each other. I am a commoner and have already brought you more than enough trouble. You'd be better off without me. Goodbye."

"Where will you go?" he called after her, but she didn't answer, just kept on walking.

"Damn it," he spat, meaning to go after her, but his cousin walked into the kitchen just then, turning to watch Maggie and her family walk out.

"What's going on?" asked Daegel.

"Maggie is running scared," he told his cousin. "She's delirious and cannot even think straight right now. I am really worried about her. I need to go after her."

"That'll have to wait," said Daegel. "Our fathers have

just returned. Brother Ruford told them what happened with your betrothed. Your father wants to have a word with you in his solar right away."

"God's eyes, can this day get any worse?" Evan stormed off, not wanting to confront his father right now. He wasn't even sure of all the details about what happened with Maggie's mother, and wasn't in any mood to try to explain it to him. His father was going to be furious to hear that he broke off the betrothal. Evan wasn't sure what to tell him or what to do.

He and Daegel walked into the solar to find both their fathers, Evan's mother, and Brother Ruford inside the room waiting for them.

"Evan," said Garrett, pacing back and forth. "Ruford tells me there was a little trouble here while I was gone."

"Father. Mother." Evan walked over to kiss his mother on the cheek. "I didn't expect you home so soon."

"The king's funeral is over, but we will be leaving again for the coronation of his nephew, Richard, soon," his father answered. "We are only here temporarily. Now, please tell me you didn't really break the betrothal I made for you."

Evan's gaze shot over to Ruford. He wasn't sure yet if the monk told his father about having torn up the papers. He decided not to push the trouble Ruford's way. He was sure his father would find out in time. "Yes, I did break the betrothal," admitted Evan. "I will not marry Lady Beatrice because I don't even know her, and after what happened today, neither do I want to."

"It was a horrible situation, my lord," said Ruford. "I have to say that I agree with Evan and even tore up the contract since it wasn't yet signed."

"Mmmph," grunted Garret. "Thank goodness I'd yet to sign it."

"Are we finished here?" asked Evan, eager to go after Maggie.

"Not yet," said his father. "Evan, why don't you tell me the real reason for all this?"

Evan looked over to Ruford and the monk couldn't meet his gaze. That told him that Ruford most likely already told his father that he was in love with Maggie. "All right, I will, even though I have a feeling Brother Ruford has already reported everything to you. I am in love with Maggie, Father. But that isn't the only reason I refuse to marry Lady Beatrice."

"Maggie?" asked Garrett.

"The midwife," Evan's mother reminded him.

"Bid the devil, please tell me you haven't fallen in love with a commoner like the rest of this mixed-up family." Garrett paced the floor. So, it seemed that Ruford had not spilled his secret after all, since his father acted as if this was the first time he was hearing about it.

Daegel's father, Corbett, laughed, crossing his arms and leaning back in his chair. "It's happening to you again, Garrett, just like it's been happening to the rest of us. I'm afraid our children will never stop marrying commoners, and that our family's namesake will be sullied for the rest of time."

"Corbett, stop it," scolded Evan's mother, Echo, who was Corbett's sister. "I believe our children should be allowed to marry whomever they want. Noble or commoner, it doesn't matter."

"And so they have," said Corbett, holding up his palms

and shrugging. "It doesn't matter what's allowed, it seems. This family goes out of their way to break all the rules and do whatever the hell they want, no matter what I say."

"What's your other reason for breaking the betrothal?" asked Evan's father curiously.

"They blamed Maggie's mother for the death of Lord Ashenden's wife and baby. They also were the ones to have Maggie's mother executed."

"They murdered a midwife?" Garrett frowned.

"Yes, Father. They are murderers. And now Maggie has taken her family and left because they've threatened to kill her and her daughter as well. She is on the run, afraid they will find her."

"What?" gasped Echo. "Did they really say that they were going to kill Maggie and the little girl?"

"They did," Daegel spoke up. "We all heard it."

"Evan, why didn't you stop Maggie from leaving?" asked his mother. "What is the matter with you? It isn't safe for her out there."

"I tried to stop her," Evan said in his defense. "I even told her I loved her, but it didn't seem to make a difference to her. She is running scared. I was about to go after her when Daegel told me that I'd been summoned by Father."

"Garrett, what are you going to do about this?" Echo demanded to know.

"Me?" Garrett scowled. "Wife, I will do nothing. Evan is the one who broke the alliance, and I think he's the one who should make amends before this starts a war between us and the Ashendens."

"You have to help them," said Evan's mother. "You are Lord Warden. Surely you can imprison the Ashendens or something for killing Maggie's mother, when we all know it was not her fault."

"Do we really know that?" asked Garrett. "This is the first I've heard about this. Evan, tell me what you know."

"I don't know much more than you, Father," Evan replied. "I had asked Maggie how her mother died, but she wouldn't tell me. I first found out when the truth came out in the courtyard with the Ashendens earlier."

"That sure sounds like guilt to me," said Corbett from his chair.

"Nay, it's not guilt," shouted Evan. "It's fear. Maggie is running scared and I will not allow her to be out there with no place to go." His hand shot upward and he pointed at the door. "For all I know, Lord Ashenden is out there right now waiting to capture Maggie and kill her like he did her mother. I cannot and will not allow that to happen."

"Let me get this straight," said his father. "Maggie's mother was the midwife tending to Lord Ashenden's wife, and she and Maggie gave birth at the same time?"

"Yes. It happened four years ago," said Evan. "Lady Beatrice said Maggie's mother tended to Maggie's birth instead of Lady Ashenden's. She said it was negligence and that was why they lost Lady Ashenden and her baby. However, I don't believe it was anyone's fault."

"I see your cause for concern," said Garrett, putting his hand to his chin in thought.

"Will you help, Father?" asked Evan.

"I don't see what I can do," his father answered. "Ashenden is out of my jurisdiction since it is not a port town. And you're telling me that Maggie's mother was executed four years ago. It has been too long. The damage is already done."

There was a knock at the door, and Evan walked over and opened it to see Giles standing there.

"What is it, squire?" he asked. "I am in the middle of something important."

"Sorry, my lord," said Giles, seeming very nervous. "There is a man and woman at the gates asking about Maggie. I saw her leave, and told them so. That's when they wanted to talk to the lord of the castle. They say it's important." Giles looked up at the others in the room. "Oh, hello, Lord Warden. I didn't know you'd returned."

"What's this all about?" Garrett walked over to join them.

"I'm not sure, but I'll find out, since it has to do with Maggie." Evan started to leave.

"Wait! I'll come with you," called out Daegel, running after him.

Evan made his way down to the courtyard to see an older man and woman standing there with worried expressions on their faces. They had a horse that was pulling a cart filled with hay.

"Are you the ones inquiring about my midwife?" asked Evan as he approached.

"Aye, my lord. I am Gertrude and this is my husband Harold," said the lady, curtsying. She elbowed her husband in the ribs and he bowed as well.

"What is this all about?" asked Daegel. "We are in the middle of something important and don't have time for nonsense."

"This isn't nonsense, my lord," said the man. "We

have been searching for Maggie Whitlock for a long time now. It was only when we heard from a traveling merchant that Saltwood Castle had a new young midwife with a brother and a young daughter that we decided it must be Maggie. We set out right away to find her."

"We've been traveling for days to get here," said the woman. "We risked everything coming here. If Lord Ashenden discovers we are missing, we will most likely be killed."

"You're from Ashenden?" Evan asked in surprise.

"Yes," said the woman. "Maggie's mother is my best friend."

"You mean she *was* your best friend," said Evan. "Maggie told me she died four years ago, and I just discovered that she was executed by Lord Ashenden."

The lady and man looked at each other oddly, but didn't answer.

"If there is something you are keeping from me, I urge you not to do so. Tell me everything you know," said Evan.

"I think it is best if we just show you." The woman looked over her shoulder at their cart. "Margaret, it is safe. You can come out now."

To Evan's surprise, a woman popped up from under the hay in the wagon, climbing out and making her way over to them.

"Margaret," Evan repeated her name, realizing she bore a striking resemblance to Maggie. "God's eyes, are you Maggie's mother?"

"I am, my lord," said the woman, lowering her head and curtsying. "Please forgive us for this intrusion but we were really hoping to find my daughter here. May I ask where she is?"

"Maggie left with her brother and daughter," said Evan. "I'm not sure where they went."

"They left?" cried Maggie's mother, looking over at Gertrude.

"We just avoided Lord Ashenden and his daughter on the road," said Gertrude. "If Maggie is out there, they are going to capture her and kill her, I'm afraid."

"How can you be sure of that?" asked Evan.

"They will, because they won't accept that what happened to Lady Ashenden and her baby was anyone's fault but mine," explained Margaret.

"I don't understand," said Evan. "I thought you were blamed for that four years ago, and executed because of it."

"It is true that they imprisoned me, but Gertrude and Harold helped me escape," said Margaret. "I ran home, but Maggie had already left with Charles and Maggie's newborn baby."

"Emma," said Evan. "Her daughter's name is Emma."

"Is it really? That was my mother's name," said Margaret, tears welling up in her eyes.

"Margaret had been badly beaten and bruised by the guards," explained Gertrude. "Harold and I hid her and nursed her back to health over the years. She was near to death, and it took a long time."

"It wasn't easy," grumbled Harold. "The castle guards kept looking for her and never let up. Several times we were almost caught."

"I need to find my daughter," cried Margaret. "She has to know that I didn't die. Please, Sir Evan, will you help us?"

"We will all help you," came the voice of Evan's mother from behind them. Evan turned to see his parents, Brother Ruford, and Lord Corbett standing there, apparently having overheard everything.

"You will all stay here under the protection of Saltwood Castle while I search for Maggie." Evan looked over at his father who didn't seem happy about this, but nodded his agreement just the same.

"Oh, thank you, my lords," said Margaret, crying. "All I have ever wanted was to be reunited with my family. I am so worried for Maggie, Charles, and little Emma. I would die if anything happened to them."

"I'll find them," Evan promised.

"And I'll help him," Daegel assured her. "We won't stop looking until they are found and safe."

"Brother Ruford, will you take our guests to the steward and get them settled in a room inside the castle?" asked Evan's mother.

"Aye, my lady. Follow me," said the monk.

"Thank you, but what about our horse and cart?" asked Harold. "I wouldn't want anything to happen to it, since that is all we own."

"My squire will take it to the stables, since he'll be readying our horses for the journey," Evan told him. "Giles, please see that two horses are prepared for me and Sir Daegel."

"I will, my lord." Giles started to go, then stopped and turned back. "Sir Evan, if you don't mind, I would like to accompany you on the search for Maggie," said the boy, surprising Evan since he knew how insecure his squire tended to be.

"You want to join us? Are you sure?" asked Evan. "It's not necessary."

"It is necessary for me, my lord," Giles told him. "You see, Maggie has always been kind to me and I respect that. I would like more than anything to repay the favor."

"Then so be it," said Evan with a smile and a nod. "I heard how you protected Maggie at the baker's, so I know you are just the person I want at my side."

"Thank you, my lord." Giles hurried away to the stables, humming. Ruford took their visitors to the keep.

"Giles is the one you want with you? Seriously?" asked Daegel, looking a little disappointed.

"And you too, of course, you simpkin." Evan swatted at Daegel, but he was fast and moved out of the way to avoid being hit."

"Guests? You called them our guests, really?" Evan heard his father say to his mother as they turned to head back to the keep as well.

"Yes, that's what they are," she replied.

"We are harboring runaways and an escaped criminal, and you call them guests." Garrett put his hand to his head as if he couldn't believe it.

"I am sure Margaret is no criminal, Garrett. Now stop being so stuffy," said Echo. "Evan and Maggie might end up getting married someday, so Margaret could very well be our future family. Get used to it."

Garrett groaned. "Why did we even return?"

"Come along, Husband. We need to decide how you are going to handle the situation to make things right with the Ashendens."

CHAPTER 14

"Thank you for the ride," said Maggie to the local vendor, getting out of the cart and picking up her travel bag, and putting Emma on the ground and holding her hand. She'd been so upset when she left the castle that she stupidly forgot her basket with everything she needed while working as a midwife. Now she'd have to buy the supplies all over again. With very little money, that would take some time. "Come along, Charles."

Charles picked up a bundle and got out of the cart as well. The sound of the horse's hooves clomped on the dirt road as the vendor left them and continued on his way.

"Maggie, why did we get out of the wagon? I don't like walking," complained Charles.

"Neither do I, but I need to stop somewhere quickly before we continue," she told him, noticing that this was the area with the brook where Maggie and Evan had spent intimate time together. She hoped to find her missing crystal pendant necklace here, thinking she might have lost it when they'd made love.

"Stop where? And what for?" asked Charles, looking around.

"If you must know, I lost my necklace when I was on an outing with Sir Evan by the brook. I think I might find it here."

"I'm tired and hungry," whined Emma.

"Me too." Charles sat down at the edge of the road and pulled out a small loaf of bread from under his cloak. "I have bread, Emma, if you want some."

"I do, I do," cried the little girl excitedly, releasing Maggie's hand and running over to Charles.

"We'll stay here and wait for you," said Charles, taking Emma onto his lap and making himself comfortable.

"Well, all right," said Maggie, scanning the area but not seeing anyone coming down the road. "I'll be quick. But if you hear anyone coming, take cover, in case it is Lord Ashenden."

"If I see another vendor, I'll ask him for a ride." Charles took a big bite of bread and then handed the loaf to Emma.

"Where did you even get that bread?" she asked her brother.

"As we were leaving the kitchen, one of those cute maids slipped it to me," said Charles proudly. "If I had a little more time, I probably could have gotten some hand-pies or sweetmeats too, but you were in too much of a hurry to leave."

"It's not that I wanted to leave, it is just that we had to go." Maggie walked toward the brook with the travel bag over her shoulder, regretting that she left Saltwood Castle so quickly. They were vulnerable out here on the road, but when they were inside the walls of the castle, they were at least safe. She was sure Evan would never hurt them. He had promised to protect them and she believed that he would. She walked toward the creek lost in deep thought.

Evan had shouted out that he loved her right before she left. It didn't really sink in, because she'd been frantic and so scared for her family that her fear overtook her, making her want to run. Did he really love her? She wondered. Or was he just saying that because he didn't want her to leave? Either way, it didn't matter she supposed. Evan had told Lord Ashenden to his face that he wouldn't marry Lady Beatrice, so she knew he wasn't lying about that.

She found the exact spot where she and Evan had made love, dropping her travel bag, taking a moment to remember how she had felt in his arms. It was the best day of her life. She'd never known anyone like Evan. He was protective, smart, handsome, and even funny. Emma had said she wanted Evan as her father, since the little girl liked him so much. Charles admired Evan since he'd been the one to get Charles the job as an apprentice locksmith. He would make a perfect father to Emma, she realized. As well as a good husband for her.

"Oh, what have I done?" moaned Maggie, sitting down in the tall grass. In her haste, she'd made a bad decision. By leaving Evan and Saltwood Castle, she'd only made her family's life worsen. Charles had just started acting like a man recently, and it was thanks to Evan. Her brother had an interest now in something besides the maids in the kitchen. She wanted more than anything to see him someday become a journeyman locksmith and make a good living.

He'd be of marrying age soon. Perhaps he'd even find a nice girl to marry.

Damn, thought Maggie. Even her younger brother would probably be married before her. She'd been holding men at a distance for years now, because she needed to be a mother to both Charles and Emma. Little Emma didn't deserve such a horrible childhood. She'd just started playing with other children, and Maggie had never seen her so happy. Now, Maggie had taken her away from her happiness.

"Why is this happening?" she asked aloud, hiding her face in her hands. Her life had been going so well since she'd met Evan. She'd found love for the first time ever. And friends. Maggie considered Ladies Martine and Eleanor her friends, even though they were nobles and she was just a commoner. How was she ever going to go on without Evan? Why had she been so stupid to leave him? She'd had the world in her hands and her family was happy for the first time in a long time, and that meant the world to her. Now she'd put them right back into despair, poverty, and sorrow, and that didn't feel good for any of them. It was all her fault, and she didn't know how to make it right.

"Oh, Mother, I've made a mistake," she mumbled into her hands. "I miss you so much and wish you were here right now so I could talk to you. This is so hard to go on. I am losing strength quickly. I just left behind a man I love. A man who loves me too. How will he ever forgive me?"

"My day has just gotten a lot better since I found you," she heard a man say, so deep in her thoughts that she hadn't even heard anyone approach.

"Evan?" she cried, jumping to her feet, realizing she'd

just made another grave mistake. "Lord Ashenden," she said, her heart lodging in her throat. He was holding the tip of his sword right at her.

"You're coming with me," he told her. "To get what you truly deserve."

Her eyes flashed back up to the road and fear coursed through her once again. She'd left Charles and Emma there by themselves, unprotected.

"Yes, we've already got the boy and the little whelp too," he said, rubbing one hand against his trews. "That little bitch bites!"

Pride filled Maggie's chest knowing that her daughter had fought back. Then it was replaced by the sinking sensation of doom for her family.

"Let's go," growled Ashenden, grabbing her roughly. Maggie struggled with him, but he was too strong for her to be able to break his hold and run. He swore at her and pushed her toward the road.

"You'd better not hurt my brother or daughter, I warn you."

"And what if I do?" he asked with a chuckle. "What are you three going to do? Your big brave knight isn't here to protect you anymore."

When they got to the road, she saw that Charles had his hands tied behind his back and was atop a horse, riding with a guard. Emma's hands were tied in front of her and she rode with Lady Beatrice.

"Mama!" cried the little girl.

"Emma!" Maggie tried to run to her daughter, but Ashenden held her back. "Tie up her hands and put her on the horse with me," he sneered. "I'd like to enjoy her curvy warm body pressed up against mine before we execute them."

"Father, that is disgusting," said Beatrice with a sniff. "Let's hurry and get back, because I cannot wait to finally punish someone for letting Mother and my baby brother die."

"You won't get away with this," ground out Charles, struggling atop the horse. The guard just held him tighter.

"Stop struggling or I'll kill you right here," warned the guard.

"Charles, do as he says," warned Maggie, trying to keep her composure. If she didn't at least pretend to be strong, Charles and Emma would be even more frightened.

The guard tied Maggie's hands and hoisted her up atop the horse with Lord Ashenden. Maggie once more looked over to the place where she and Evan had made love, and felt like crying. It had been a dream come true but it just turned into a terrible nightmare.

"That's right, take a good, long, last look," said Ashenden, blowing his breath in her ear since they were sitting so close. Just the smell of his breath and the fact he was pressed up against her made her want to vomit. "Take a last look, because it'll be the last thing you ever see."

"So you say you saw a vendor with a woman, little girl, and a boy in the back of his cart?" Evan asked from atop his horse to two washwomen walking along the road carrying baskets of laundry.

"Aye, my lord," said the short, plump woman.

"How long ago?" asked Daegel.

"Not long," said the skinny one.

"Did it seem they were being taken against their will?" asked Evan.

"Nay, my lord," said the first woman. "They seemed like they wanted to be there."

"They even waved to us and the little girl called out hello," said the second.

"Which way did they go?" asked Giles.

"Straight up the road that way." The plump woman pointed down the road.

"Take a left at the fork in the road," instructed her friend.

"Thank you," said Evan, reaching into his pouch and pulling out two coins and tossing the money to them. "You've been ever so helpful."

"Thank you, my lord," both women called out, dropping their baskets and falling to their knees to pick up the coins.

"Do you think we'll find them, my lord?" asked Giles, as they continued to ride. "It'll be getting dark soon."

"We'll find them," Evan replied, trying to stay positive.

"They couldn't have gone far," said Daegel.

It wasn't long before they came across a vendor with his wagon traveling slowly down the road.

"Stop," called out Evan, riding to the man's side.

"My lord." The man stopped his wagon and bowed his head. "Did I do something wrong?" Evan looked to the back of the wagon but there seemed to only be goods the man was selling. Maggie and the others were not there. "Did you give a ride to a blonde woman, a boy, and a little girl?"

"Yes, my lord," said the man. "I did."

"Where are they now?"

"I dropped them off back there by the brook," he told them. "It was where the woman said she wanted to go."

"Thank you," said Evan, giving him a coin as well. He rode back to Daegel and Giles.

"Did he see them?" asked Daegel.

"He gave them a ride, but we need to go back. He said he left them at the brook."

"What brook?" asked Daegel.

"We'll never find them," said Giles. "It is wooded and the grass is tall."

"Nay, I know exactly where they went," Evan told the others, taking off at breakneck speed down the road. He was sure that for some reason Maggie had gone back to the place where they'd made love. He hoped she was still there, because it would be night soon like Giles said, and he knew how Maggie hated traveling alone at night.

Evan approached the spot where they'd made love, seeing something half hidden in the tall grass. "I found something," he called out to the others. Jumping off his horse he ran forward, hoping it was not a dead body. He pushed the tall grass aside, seeing a travel bag.

"What is it, my lord?" asked Giles.

"Is it Maggie?" Daegel jumped off his horse and ran over to Evan.

"It's her travel bag," he said, not needing to open it to look inside to know. He'd seen her packing it and was sure it was hers.

"So they were here, then," said Giles.

"Yes. Spread out. See what else you can find," Evan instructed.

They searched for a while but couldn't find anyone or anything else.

"Why in the world would they come here?" asked Giles.

Evan walked directly up to the spot where they'd made love. The grass was still tamped down from when they'd laid on it. "This is where we made love," he said softly.

"Oh. Oooooh," said Giles, his face reddening. He got off his horse and went over to pick up Maggie's travel bag.

Looking to the ground, Evan saw something reflect in the light of the setting sun. He bent down and picked it up, realizing it was Maggie's crystal pendant. She must have lost it the day they'd made love and had come back to look for it.

"What did you find?" asked Daegel, stretching his neck to see.

"Did you find something else?" shouted Giles, running over with the bag to join them. "Oh, that is Maggie's good luck charm, isn't it?"

"Yes," said Evan. "Maggie told me that it used to be her mother's pendant. Her mother gave it to her when she was pregnant with Emma. It always brought her mother good luck, and her mother wanted her to have good luck too."

"Well, it doesn't seem as if she's going to have good luck without it," said Daegel, stretching his neck again. "Look over there. I see something else."

They walked over to inspect what Daegel had pointed out.

"There is a lot of broken brush here," Giles noticed.

"I see footprints too." Daegel pointed to the ground. Sure enough there were two sets of footprints. One of them being larger than the other.

"It looks like a man and a woman," said Evan. "It almost seems as if there was a struggle by the way the footprints intersect and dig down into the soil."

"Do you think it was Maggie?" asked Giles.

"Maggie and a man she didn't want to be with, by the looks of this," said Evan.

"Yes, she could have been abducted, since I highly doubt she'd leave her bag," said Giles.

"Nay. She wouldn't leave it," said Evan. "Not when it's all she had, and she needs to take care of her family."

Daegel walked a little farther and found a scrap of torn clothing caught on a branch. He picked it up with two fingers and inspected it. "This is made of wool, but the cloth is not coarse like a commoner's. It must be from a noble's cloak," he said aloud, rubbing the fabric between two fingers. "An odd color choice, though. Nobles don't usually wear this shade of green."

"Daegel, we've seen that color before, if you don't remember. That is from the cloak of Lord Ashenden or his daughter, I am sure of it. They are the only ones I've ever seen wearing murky moat green. They have abducted Maggie and her family!"

CHAPTER 15

The door to the dungeon cell clanked closed, and the guard turned the key in the lock leaving Maggie, Charles, and Emma in the dank, smelly, cold cell without even a blanket, water, or food.

"Lucky you, that it's already night," the guard said in a sarcastic tone. "Lord Ashenden has decided he's tired and that you'll all be hanged in the morning instead."

"That's right." Lady Beatrice appeared behind the guard. Her long cloak swept over the floor as she walked. "Your mother might have escaped four years ago, but mark my words, you three won't. You'll die in her place for the death of my mother."

"Escape?" Maggie couldn't believe what she'd just heard. She held Emma in her arms, walking closer to the cell door. Emma whimpered, hiding her face against Maggie's chest. "What do you mean my mother escaped? You killed her."

"I tried to kill her but someone helped her escape before

I could do it," Lady Beatrice told her. "We've been searching for her for years, just like we've been looking for you and your whelp." She shot a nasty glance at Emma, making the little girl cry. "Who would have thought we'd be lucky enough to find you at the castle of my betrothed."

"Evan is not your betrothed. He loves me," cried Maggie.

"If he loves you, then where is he now?" Beatrice stuck her nose in the air.

"Evan won't let us die," shouted Charles, reaching out and shaking the bars of the cell door. "He cares about us too much. He'll come save us."

"I hope he tries," said Beatrice. "Then he can watch each one of you die in the morning."

"Nay!" cried Maggie. "Don't kill my brother and daughter. Take me if you want, but leave them alone. They had nothing to do with this."

"Nothing to do with this?" asked the woman. "Because of your daughter, my brother died. If your mother hadn't been helping you birth her, she would have been doing her job and helping my mother instead."

"Please. Let them go. I'll stay here and you can do what you want to me, but do not harm them in any way, I beg you. They are my family."

"Stop your begging, because your little family is going to die right alongside you. Now shut up before I have my guard rough you up." Beatrice turned and left. The guard followed.

There was only one wall torch lighting the dungeon, and it was flickering and threatening to go out as well. The floor was cold and wet. The smell of urine and rotting flesh filled the air.

"I'm scared, Mama," said Emma, clinging to Maggie. The

little girl reached under her traveling cloak and pulled out Elizabeth's soggy doll and hugged her.

"Where did that come from?" Maggie asked in surprise, knowing that Lord Ashenden had taken all their things.

"I hid the dolly under my cape so she'd be safe," said Emma. "I'm going to protect her because she is scared too."

"Don't be frightened, Emma. Evan will save us." Maggie walked to the side of the cell, jumping when a hand came through the bars and someone grabbed her arm.

"You're a pretty young thing," came the gravelly voice of the prisoner in the next cell. He was an older man, with rotten teeth and a big scar across his face. "How about a kiss?"

"Leave me alone!" Maggie tried to pull away, but the man's fingers gripped her arm tightly.

"Let go of my mama!" Emma, still in Maggie's arms, used Elizabeth's doll and started beating it against the man's hand.

"Nay!" cried Charles, rushing across the floor of the cell to help. He grabbed the prisoner's arm, squeezing tightly while Emma kept beating him with the doll. Finally, the man released Maggie. She hurried to the center of the cell and sat down with Emma on her lap.

"Are you all right, Maggie?" asked her brother.

"I'm fine," she said, seeing scratch marks on her arm, but thankfully the skin was not broken. She didn't even have her creams and ointment to help heal them if they got hurt. "Thank you both for coming to my aid."

"Mama, my dolly broke," cried Emma, holding out the doll to show her that its head was hanging off, held on only by a wire that ran through the center of the doll.

"Oh, Emma, I am sure we can fix her. Once we get back to the castle, I will sew her up," she said, trying to make it sound as if they were going to go back to Saltwood instead of to the gallows in the morning.

"Let me see that," said Charles, taking the doll from Emma.

"Can you fix it, Charlie?" asked Emma, looking up at him with sad eyes.

Charles fiddled with the doll's head and grinned. "I think I can do something better." He yanked the doll's head off in one quick motion, causing Emma to scream out and then cry.

"Charlie killed my doll," wailed Emma, hiding her head against Maggie's chest again.

"Charles! Why did you do that?" snapped Maggie, feeling that things were bad enough without her brother ripping apart a little girl's doll.

"I did it because I need this." He pulled out a long wire, throwing the doll to the side.

"What on earth?" Emma looked at her brother thinking the boy had gone mad.

"I have an idea of how we can get out of here."

"With a wire?" asked Maggie.

"Exactly." Charles stood up, twisting the wire, walking over to the door of the cell. He glanced over to the guard station, and then when he was sure no one was watching, he stuck his hand through the bars, pushing the wire into the padlock, jigging it back and forth.

"What on earth are you doing?" Maggie got up carrying Emma, and walked over to the cell door.

"Shhh, I need to listen," he told her, twisting the wire in

the lock until she heard a small click. Then he looked back at her and smiled, giving the door a slight nudge. To her utter astonishment, it opened.

"Charles, you are brilliant!" she whispered, continuously looking back at the guard station so they wouldn't be spotted.

"I learned a few tricks, being a locksmith's apprentice," Charles boasted.

"I suppose you did."

"What's all that noise about in there?" shouted the guard, sticking his head out from the guard's station. "Go to sleep or I'll knock you out to make you do it."

"Can you do that again?" Maggie whispered to her brother.

"I'm sure I can. Why?"

"Close the door," she told him. "We'll wait until the guard falls asleep and then we'll move forward with our plan to escape."

"Why are we coming back to the castle instead of going to Ashenden?" asked Daegel, as they rode through the gates just as the sun set.

"Because, there is someone I need to speak to first," said Evan.

Evan got off his horse, handing the reins to the stableboy and hightailing it to the great hall. Daegel and Giles were right behind him.

"My lord, I don't understand," said Giles. "Aren't we going to find and save Maggie?"

"Of course we are, but there is something I need to know first."

Evan entered the great hall just as the meal was taking place. His father, mother, and the other nobles were up at the dais table where the nobles ate. Even Martine and Eleanor were eating there today. Everyone else was seated below the salt.

"Evan, Evan!" Eleanor waved to him, calling him over. The men went to the dais. "Did you find Maggie and the others?" asked his sister.

"Nay, not yet. But I know where they are."

"Where?" asked his mother, overhearing them.

"We found her travel bag at the creek," said Daegel.

"That's right," said Evan. "Along with this." He dug into his bag and held up her crystal.

"Her lucky necklace," gasped Martine. "She should have it with her. That's not good."

Evan slipped the necklace back into his pouch. "We also found evidence that tells me that Maggie and her brother and daughter have been abducted by Lord Ashenden."

"And so the battle has begun," said his father under his breath.

"Father, this has nothing to do with me breaking the betrothal," Evan told him.

"Doesn't it?" asked Garrett.

"Nay," said Evan, becoming very frustrated that his father would even say that. "It is because of what happened in Maggie's past."

"Sir Evan, did you find my daughter?" Margaret ran up, with her friends right behind her.

"Margaret, I believe she's been abducted with the others and that Lord Ashenden has her," Evan told the woman.

"Nay!" cried Margaret. "He will kill them! Oh, this is all my fault. I never should have escaped."

"Speaking of that, I need to know exactly how you were able to escape the dungeon of Ashenden Castle," said Evan.

"My friends helped me." Margaret looked over to Gertrude and Harold.

"There is a secret entrance to the dungeon that is not guarded," explained Gertrude. "My father helped build it long ago. Not many know about it since it isn't used anymore."

"Where exactly is it?" asked Evan. "I need to get in there and quickly."

"You'll need keys to the cell if you're going to release Maggie and her family," stated Harold. "Four years ago, I lifted the ring of keys from a guard when he fell asleep. But since Margaret's escape, Lord Ashenden makes certain there are always at least two guards so that won't happen again. There is always a guard awake to watch the prisoners now."

"Don't worry. Just help me get in there and I'll figure out a way," said Evan, feeling like he was wasting time and every minute counted. For all he knew, Maggie and her family could already be dead. "Explain to me where to find this secret entrance."

"We'll do better than that," said Gertrude. "We'll come with you and show you."

"Yes," cried Margaret. "Me too. I'd do anything to help my family."

"I know you would, but none of you will be coming with me," Evan told them. "There are already enough lives at stake and I won't have you risk yours. Daegel and Giles and I will handle this by ourselves."

"Garrett, you should go with them," said Evan's mother.

"I would, but you know I can't," his father answered. "If I show up, it will definitely be considered an act of war. Besides, we leave first thing in the morning for Richard's coronation. I have to be there, Echo. Evan is a knight now. He will be able to figure this out by himself. I have every bit of confidence in him, so stop worrying."

"Father is right," Evan told his mother. "This is something that I am meant to do."

Daegel cleared his throat. "*We* are meant to do," he told Evan. "After all, I can't let you get all the credit." He flashed Evan a smile.

"Thank you," said Evan softly, knowing his cousin was his true friend.

"Evan," said Garrett as Evan turned to leave. "I hope you find Maggie and her family alive. I really mean that."

"I hope so more than anyone, Father."

"I may not be able to go there personally, but I will send messenger pigeons at once to the rest of your uncles. Mayhap they can help."

"Thank you, but it's not necessary," said Evan, figuring that was not going to do a bit of good. After all, by the time his uncles even got the missives, Maggie could be dead. Not to mention, his Uncle Storm MacKeefe was a Scot and lived over the border. "Let's talk," Evan told Harold and Gertrude. "I need to know everything about Ashenden Castle, because I am going to go in and save Maggie and her family tonight or die trying."

CHAPTER 16

"We're never going to be able to escape because they keep switching out the guards for new ones." Charles watched from the front of the cell. "They also keep two guards posted, so they're never going to fall asleep. Mayhap this is a bad idea after all."

"Nay," Maggie told him. "We've got to try something to save ourselves." Maggie held her sleeping daughter in her arms. She'd finally been able to get Emma to stop crying and go to sleep. The little girl held tightly to the broken doll, hugging it like a lifeline. Maggie could only hope the wire from that doll really would prove to be a lifeline. They needed to get out of here before morning or they were all going to lose their lives, and she could not allow that to happen.

Maggie kept hoping to see Evan coming to their rescue. But since he didn't even know where they were, that was going to be more of a dream than reality. She couldn't blame him. She was the one who left and never even gave him a chance to talk with her. Especially after he'd told her that he loved her, and she had been too upset to tell him that she loved him too.

"Mayhap I can knock out the guards so we can get past," said Charles, pacing the floor of the cell.

"Nay, Charles. It is too risky. I don't want you to get hurt. If you go up against an armed guard, they'll most likely kill you tonight after all."

"Maggie, I'm scared," said Charles. "Are we really going to die here? All of us?"

"Nay, of course not," she said, wanting to believe it was true but not seeing how they were going to get out of his horrible situation. "We just need to come up with a plan to stall the execution until Evan arrives."

Charles looked forlorn. "He's not really coming, is he?"

"I will never give up hope and neither should you. Now, let's think. What can we do?"

They waited until there was only one guard out in the outer room while the other left to be switched out. It was late into the night and they'd only have a few minutes before another guard arrived. Maggie looked over to Charles, feeling so scared because this was either going to work or get them killed earlier than planned. Still, they had to try something.

"Are you ready?" she asked, having used their cloaks rolled up to make a fake person which she'd placed in the shadows of the cell against the back wall. It was too dark to see that it wasn't really Charles lying on the floor, unless a guard would actually come into the cell to look.

"As ready as I'll ever be," Charles told her, using the wire to pick the lock once more. The lock twanged and her heart jumped. Maggie's eyes shot back to the guard's room but thankfully the guard hadn't seemed to hear it. "Here I go," he whispered, slipping out of the cell and slowly closing the door almost all the way, making sure to leave it open just a crack.

The plan was that Charles would hide in the shadows while Maggie called the guard over, telling him that Charles was ill. When the guard walked up, Maggie would throw the door open, hitting the guard to distract him, while Charles took the heavy torch from the wall and hit the man over the head, knocking him out. Then Maggie would join Charles with Emma, and somehow they'd sneak out of the castle, hopefully before the replacement guard showed up.

It might not be the best plan, she realized, but it was all they had right how.

"Call him over," mouthed Charles from the shadow.

"All right," she whispered back. She still held her sleeping daughter in her arms. She'd have to carry Emma out of here, and prayed that the little girl wouldn't wake up and start crying and alarm the rest of the castle. "Oh, guard!" she called out. "My brother is ill. Please, he needs help. Come quickly."

Unfortunately, speaking so loudly woke up her daughter. Emma stirred.

"Is Charlie sick, Mama?" Emma looked over at the bundle of cloaks on the floor across the cell.

"Shhh, Emma. Close your eyes and go back to sleep," she told the little girl. "Stay quiet."

"What's all the shouting about?" grumbled the guard, coming to the cell.

Maggie saw Charles sneak over to the torch.

"It's my brother. He's ill and needs your help," said Maggie.

Emma's head popped up and she looked around.

The guard came closer, and Maggie glanced back at Charles and almost died. He was trying his hardest, but couldn't get the torch out of the wall. He tugged and pulled but it wouldn't budge. Without the torch they'd have nothing to use to hit the guard over the head. She didn't think things could get worse, but of course they did.

"Is that door unlocked?" asked the guard, at the same time Emma spotted Charles and called out.

"Look, Mama, Charlie is outside the cell over there." She pointed to Maggie's brother. The guard spun around drawing his sword.

"What the hell," the guard ground out.

Still holding Emma with one arm, Maggie took a hold of the cell door with the other and pushed it hard into the guard.

"Ooomph," spat the guard, stumbling forward. However, he never dropped his sword. "Prisoner escape!" the guard shouted, going after Charles.

"Nay! Leave him alone!" shouted Maggie, lunging from the cell with a crying Emma in her arms.

"Maggie, help me!" screamed Charles, putting his hands over his head as the guard's sword came down right at him.

"It's not nice to fight an unarmed boy," came a voice from the dark. To Maggie's surprise, Evan emerged from the shadows, grabbing the guard's raised sword from behind him. The guard spun around, pulling his sword with him and raising it up toward Evan now. Evan used his sword to block the guard's blow.

"Evan!" Maggie shouted, just as a dozen more guards stormed in through the door. It was almost as if they knew Maggie and her family would try to escape and they were waiting to ambush them. Each guard had their sword raised, ready to attack. "Watch out!" she cried.

Evan's sword clashed with that of a guard, and two more dark figures shot out of the shadows to help him.

"The odds against us are looking grim," said Daegel, fighting alongside Evan.

"Watch out, my lord," cried Giles, stopping a blow as the sword was about to sink into Evan.

"Maggie, come on." Charles was at the door, waving her to him. "Sir Evan came in through some secret entrance. We can escape through there while they're fighting the guards."

Maggie stepped out of the cell with Emma in her arms. The broken doll hung from Emma's fingers. The little girl was so scared that she stopped crying and hid her face against Emma, hugging the doll once again.

"Is Sir Evan going to die?" asked Emma, her face still pressed up against Maggie.

"Shhh," said Maggie, not wanting to draw more attention to themselves.

"Maggie, take your family and leave. Quickly," shouted Evan as he continued to fight. "There is a secret entrance at the far end of the dungeon."

"Nay. I won't leave you, Evan. I love you," she screamed.

"Now is a hell of a time to tell me," he mumbled, using the hilt of his sword to knock out a guard. Still, it was a dozen against three, and Maggie couldn't see how they were all going to walk out of here with their lives.

"Let us out and we'll help you fight them," begged the

seedy man who had grabbed her arm through the bars earlier.

"You tried to hurt me," said Maggie. "Why should I trust you?"

"We will all help," called out another man, followed by all the prisoners offering to help her. Maggie looked down the row of cells where the prisoners were all sticking their arms out through the bars, begging her not to leave them.

"You are all prisoners," said Charles. "You belong behind bars."

"Just like you, right?" asked one of the men. His words hit Maggie hard as she thought about her mother. Innocent people sometimes were executed and she knew that was the truth.

"They're going to execute us all in the morning," said another. "At least give us a chance to help you and possibly save our own lives too."

"Come on, Maggie, let's go." Charles tried to pull her out of there, but Maggie wasn't going to leave unless she knew Evan and the others were safe. She also felt bad for the prisoners. Mayhap this truly was the answer.

"Nay, Charles. Open the locks of all the cells, quickly. Let them all out."

"What?" Charles blinked in confusion. "They're cutthroats and bandits, Maggie. You can't mean that."

"We don't know that. They might have been falsely accused just like us or like our mother. Let them help fight and try to save their own lives at the same time. If not, we all might be dead soon."

"Yes. Listen to her," cried the man who had grabbed Maggie."

"These prisoners have just as much a right to live as anyone else."

"I suppose you're right," said Charles, managing to get the rings of keys from the guard and quickly unlocking one door after another, letting the prisoners escape. "Besides, we need to help Sir Evan."

The escaped prisoners rushed out and helped Evan, Daegel, and Giles fight the guards just as they'd promised.

"What's this?" Evan turned around in surprise.

"They're helping," Charles called out, finding another torch that wasn't lit and pulling it out of the stone wall. Then he rushed forward into the commotion and hit a guard over the head and knocked him out. "I did it!" shouted Charles.

"Try not to kill any of them," Evan called out.

"Why not?" snarled a prisoner. "They were going to kill us."

"You kill them and you'll be wanted for murder," Evan told them. "I have a better idea."

Maggie watched as Evan worked with the prisoners, Charles, Giles, and Daegel. They managed to knock out or capture all the guards without any of them or any of the prisoners being killed.

"Shove the guards into the cells and lock them inside," commanded Evan.

"Great idea, Cousin," said Daegel with a chuckle.

When all the guards were imprisoned, Evan waved his hand over his head. "There is a secret passage where all of you can escape," he told the prisoners. "Follow me."

"Wait. I want a sword," said one prisoner, picking up the blade.

"I'll take this dagger," said another.

"If you take weapons, I warn you not to use them unless it is a last resort and in self-defense," Evan called out. "You are all on your own now. Good luck."

"Evan, you came for us," cried Maggie, running to him with Emma still in her arms. She gave him a hug and a kiss.

"There will be time for this later, sweetheart." Evan directed her toward the secret passageway. "Right now, my only concern is to get my family home safely."

"Y-your family?" asked Maggie, so choked with emotion that she could barely speak.

"That's right," said Evan. "Because as soon as we get back to Saltwood Castle, I am going to marry you and make you my wife."

"Really? I'd like that," she told him.

He bent over and kissed her with passion and then turned her around and helped her to the secret passage. Maggie didn't remember another thing until they were atop the horses and headed home, because thoughts filled her head of being married to Evan and it made her feel safe and happy all over again.

CHAPTER 17

Maggie rode atop Evan's horse with him, while Charlie rode with Daegel and Emma with Giles on their way back to the castle. Traveling in the dark never felt so safe and secure as it did right now. She was back in Evan's arms again, and this is exactly where she wanted to be.

"I thought I'd lost you," he said, his mouth up against her ear. He kissed her earlobe, making her smile.

"I thought you'd never show up," she said with a giggle, turning to see his frown. "I'm only jesting," she said, cupping his cheek in her hand and kissing him hard on the mouth.

"Mmmmph," he said, getting that lusty look in his eyes again. "Save that for the bedchamber, darling."

"Evan, thank you for coming to save us."

"Did you think I'd let you die?"

"I hoped not. However, I thought my luck ran out since I lost my good luck charm."

"Oh, that reminds me." He pulled something out of his side pouch and dangled it in front of her face.

"My crystal!" she exclaimed, taking it from him and putting the cord around her neck. "Where did you find it?"

"Right where you lost it. By the brook where we made love."

"Evan, are you serious about wanting me to be your wife?"

"I am. I told you that I love you, Maggie."

"I love you, too. But you are a noble and I am only a commoner."

"I don't care. I want to be with you for the rest of my life."

She smiled, feeling happier than she ever thought she could.

"Maggie?" he asked.

"Yes?" She looked back at him.

"You haven't said yes to my proposal yet."

"I didn't think I needed to, since you know how I feel about you."

"Then you'll be my wife?"

"I would be honored to be your wife, Evan. It would make me very happy." She reached up and kissed him once again.

They arrived at the castle and rode through the gates. The courtyard was crowded, as if everyone was waiting for them to return.

"Maggie?" a woman called out.

She looked down to see her mother.

"Mother! You really are alive." She started to dismount but Evan stopped her.

"You are tired and weak and I insist you let me help you from the horse." He got off and helped her down.

Maggie fell into her mother's arms, crying in joy.

"Mother!" Charles jumped off the horse before it stopped moving, and ran over and hugged their mother as well.

"Charles!" exclaimed Margaret. "You've grown so much that I barely recognize you. Let me look at you," she said, standing back to drink in the sight. "My, you are a man already. I feel like I missed so much." Charles stood a little straighter, liking that his mother had called him a man.

"Maggie, Emma wants you," said Giles, walking over and handing her daughter to her.

"Oh! Is that my granddaughter? I haven't seen her since the day she was born." Maggie's mother put her hands to her mouth and started crying.

"Yes, Mother. This is Emma. Emma, this is your grand-mother," Maggie introduced them.

"I have a grandmother? Like Elizabeth has one?" asked the little girl.

"Yes, sweetheart, that's right. Now give your grand-mother a hug." Maggie handed Emma over to her mother. Her mother hugged and kissed Emma, making Emma giggle.

"I never want to let you go. Ever," said Margaret, hugging the child tightly.

"Hello, Maggie," came a voice, and Maggie looked over to see her old friends.

"Gertrude! Harold! I've missed you two," she said, hugging the woman and then the man. "Thank you both for saving my mother. Evan told me all about it."

. . .

Evan watched the little family reunion, feeling emotional as well.

"You're not going to cry, are you?" Daegel said softly from next to him. "After all, you're a knight now, and knights don't cry."

"Remind yourself of that in a minute after I punch you in the gut, and we'll find out for sure if that is true," Evan jested.

"Sir Evan!" Brother Ruford ran out of the keep with Ladies Martine and Eleanor with him.

"Maggie!" Martine got to Maggie first, giving her a huge hug.

"We're so glad you are all right. All of you," said Eleanor, looking over to Evan. She came over and gave him a kiss on the cheek.

"Where are Mother and Father?" asked Evan.

"We're here," called out his mother, holding up the hem of her long skirt and running over to wrap her arms around Evan. "My prayers have been answered that you are all alive and have returned."

"Welcome back, Son. Good job," said Garrett, slapping Evan on the back. "How did you do it?"

Evan answered. "Let's just say that in the morning, Lord Ashenden and his daughter are going to have a little surprise to find their guards all locked in the cells and all their prisoners missing."

"Did you kill any of them?" asked Garrett.

"Nay."

"Good," said Garrett. "Then this will be easier than I thought."

"What will be easier, Father?"

"I sent messenger pigeons to not only your uncles, but to Windsor Castle as well."

"Why? I don't understand," said Evan.

"Let's just say Maggie won't have to worry about Lord Ashenden and his daughter coming after her family ever again."

"Why not?"

"I have some friends on the Regent Council and I was able to work things out," Garrett explained. "Come morning, Lord Ashenden is being sent to France to fight for the new king. His daughter is being sent with him. And ... they're never coming back to England. Or at least that is what I've been told."

"Really?" Evan raised a brow. "That is better news than I could have asked for. Thank you, Father, for getting involved, after all."

"I wasn't going to abandon you, Son. I just wanted to help out in my own way."

"And if you didn't, I'm sure Mother would have taken up her sword again and gone after the Ashendens herself, right?"

"I didn't want to wait to find out," said Garrett, looking over at his wife and smiling. Both the men laughed about it since they knew it was probably true.

"Father, I want to marry Maggie," Evan announced. "I have already asked her and she agreed to be my wife."

"I think that is wonderful," said his mother, overhearing their conversation. "Congratulations. And by the way, yes, I wouldn't have hesitated to pick up my sword and help you, Evan, if your father hadn't all but held me down."

"All is well that ends well," said Garrett.

"Father? What are your thoughts on me marrying Maggie?" Evan wanted to get back to the subject of marrying Maggie. He wanted his father's approval since he respected the man and didn't want to be on bad terms. He held his breath, hoping his father wouldn't object.

"Why shouldn't I be surprised?" asked Garrett. "It seems to be the trend in this family to marry from below the salt."

"Then you approve?"

"Do you love each other?"

"We do."

"Then what can I say?"

"Husband, you can tell him you approve so he stops holding his breath." Echo scowled at her husband.

"Congratulations, Son. I approve," said Garrett, holding out his hand and shaking Evan's. "I only ask that you wait to have the wedding ceremony until your mother and I return from the king's coronation."

"And until we can send out messenger pigeons out, telling all the relatives so they can join us too," added his mother.

"Our relatives? All of them?" asked Evan, thinking how overwhelming this would be for Maggie. "That's not necessary."

"It is unless you want to hear a lot of complaining from all your female cousins and sister, not to mention your mother," said his father.

"Then we'll marry when you return," Evan told him with

a smile, even though he didn't want to wait another minute to make Maggie Whitlock his wife.

"I'm sorry about Elizabeth's doll, and I will replace it," Maggie told Eleanor the next day in the great hall, feeling bad that Emma had not only swiped the doll from Eleanor's daughter, but that it got ruined in the dungeon as well.

"This doll?" Evan walked up to them, holding up the doll that was not only fixed but looked clean and like brand-new.

"My dolly," said Emma, jumping up and down trying to get it.

"It's not yours, Emma. "It is Elizabeth's," Maggie reminded her.

"Elizabeth is too young to miss it," said Eleanor. "I think Emma should have it. After all, I heard how that doll helped you to escape the dungeon."

"Yes, this doll is very good at what she does." Evan scooped up Emma and gave it to her.

"Thank you for fixing her, Father." Emma kissed Evan on the cheek.

"He's not your father yet, sweetheart," Maggie explained. "Not until we get married."

"I'm going to call him my Father now because I want to, and I've never had a father before." Emma wasn't going to give it up.

"It's all right," he told her. "But I want you to know that I had a little help fixing up ... Erszba."

"Who?" Maggie laughed.

"Erszba," said Evan, nodding to the doll that Maggie hugged. "After all, she is part of the family too so I thought her name should start with an E."

"I hope you are not going to want to name our future children anything so ... odd-sounding."

"Well, there are only so many names that start with E, and my family is using them up quickly." Evan shrugged and laughed, making Maggie love him even more.

"So, who helped you fix the doll?" asked Maggie. "Daegel?"

"Nay. Daegel wouldn't be caught dead holding a doll. It was your mother."

"That's right," said Maggie's mother from behind her. "And I am going to make dolls for every one of my grandchildren. Lots and lots of dolls for lots and lots of grandchildren. Look. I've already started." Margaret held up two more dolls made of rags to show them.

"Mother, we are not even married yet," Maggie told her. "Slow down."

"Please don't make our boys dolls too, or Daegel will never let me live this down," said Evan.

"I promise," said Maggie's mother. "And I wasn't talking about your future children, but my other grandchildren. These dolls are for Elizabeth and one for Eleanor's next baby, who I think is going to be a girl."

"Eleanor is pregnant again?" asked Evan in surprise.

"Yes," said Margaret. "I examined her myself and it is true."

"Did she tell Connor yet?" asked Maggie.

"She did and he is thrilled. Come, Emma. You and I are going to pass out Erszba's friends to your cousins." She took

Emma from Evan and walked away, chatting happily with her granddaughter.

"I have a feeling my mother is never going to let either one of us hold Emma again."

"Well," said Evan with a shrug. "Then I suggest we start making more babies as soon as possible, so we have a shot at holding them once in a while."

"Soon?" Maggie looked at him from the side of her eyes. "How soon?"

"How does right now sound?"

"Now? Really?" Excitement coursed through her.

"Well, your mother is taking care of Emma, and Daegel took Charles to the blacksmith's shop in town. Charles has not only taken a sudden interest in being a locksmith, but he's met the blacksmith's very pretty daughter, and has a second interest now as well."

"I see." Maggie took his arm. "Charles is definitely a man now, like Mother said."

"I guess so."

"Where did you want to start making all these babies, Sir Evan? In the mews, or perhaps the bakehouse, or mayhap in the moat? After all, you seem to like wild, new, exciting places."

"Any place with you is exciting," he told her, escorting her to the keep. "However, I think right now I would like to make love to my bride-to-be in the normal way in a normal place—my bed."

"Sounds good to me," she said with a giggle, as they hurried to Evan's bedchamber, rushing inside and closing the door behind them.

. . .

Evan wanted Maggie so badly that they didn't even make it to the bed. He pulled off her clothes right there, kissing her, fondling her all the while. Maggie was feeling just as excited as he, because she did the same to him.

"Evan, I can't believe we are doing this in the middle of the day." Maggie kissed him, her arms closing around his neck.

"Middle of the day? It's only morning, sweetheart." He scooped her off her feet, causing her to squeal and then cover her mouth.

"I'm sorry. I'll try to be quieter." She wrapped her legs around Evan's waist and held on to him as he reached forward to suckle her breast.

"Why bother?" he asked, when he came up for air. "Everyone knows we'll be married within the next few weeks. and I've already had Brother Ruford post the wedding banns. We have nothing to be ashamed of, so relax and have fun."

"Evan, I want you so bad right now that I don't think I can wait any longer."

"I'm ready," he told her, his erection pressed hard against her. "Check if you don't believe me."

She reached down and wrapped her fingers around his manhood, making him instantly harder than he already was.

"Mmmm," he grunted, sliding inside her from his standing position.

"Oh!" she gasped. "Can you really make love to me this way?"

"Watch me," he said, kissing her and walking over to the

wall, putting her back against it to steady her while he thrust in and out.

She cried out in excitement, the smile on her face as her eyes closed and she looked up to the ceiling, telling him that Maggie had just found another way she enjoyed making love.

"I want you to be comfortable so I'm taking you to the bed," he said through ragged breaths, feeling as if he were about to explode with desire.

"I love you," she told him, as he climbed atop her and positioned himself between her legs.

"I love you, too, Maggie." He entered her then, and they made hot, passionate love in the normal way. They coupled with such force and passion that the bed ropes holding up the pallet creaked and eventually broke. They ended up on the ground atop the pallet, laughing.

"If this is any indication of what is to come, then I think we're going to be having many babies, just like my mother wants," Maggie told him.

"How many children *do* you want, Maggie?"

"Many, many," she said with a smile. "After all, I am a midwife and I have been helping women birth babies for most of my life. I think it is time some of those babies are mine now."

"I agree," he told her. "As long as at least six of them are sons." He winked and kissed her again, knowing that he would be happy with sons or daughters and would love them all just as much. As long as their mother was his beautiful, precious Maggie.

CHAPTER 18
THREE WEEKS LATER

The day of the wedding was here and Maggie felt so anxious that she thought she was going to retch.

"Maggie?" said her mother, coming into the ladies' solar where Ladies Eleanor and Martine were helping her finish dressing. "Everyone is ready for the ceremony. Are you?"

"I suppose so," she said, her hand going to her stomach. "I am so jittery that I feel ill."

"Ill?" asked her mother.

"Yes, her stomach has been upset for the last week," said Martine. Martine and Eleanor were acting as Maggie's bridesmaids today, while Emma was going to throw petals of flowers out in front of Maggie as she walked to the altar.

"Maggie, when is the last time you had your flux?" asked her mother with a grin.

"It was ... oh, I suppose I did miss one," said Maggie, understanding what her mother meant. "Do you think I'm ... pregnant?" It was such a wonderful thought that Maggie was almost afraid to say it aloud.

"I've been a midwife for a long time, Daughter, and yes, my guess is that you are," answered her mother.

"Oh, Maggie, congratulations," said Martine. "Our children will all be playing together soon."

"Mayhap she'll have twins like you," Eleanor chimed in.

"Twins?" Suddenly Maggie started picturing having not only twins, but even triplets. Multiple births seemed to run in this family. She supposed it would be all right. After all, if she was going to have six sons like Evan wanted, it would mean she'd be pregnant a lot. Having them a few at a time might be easier.

"You have made me so very happy, Maggie." Her mother gave her a hug. "I am the luckiest woman in the world."

"Luck?" Maggie's hand went to her crystal. "That reminds me, Mother. I want to give you back your lucky necklace."

"Nay, you keep it," said her mother, raising her hand in the air. "You might need it birthing all those babies that you and Evan will be having. Plus, you can give it to Emma when it is her time to be a midwife or for her to give birth."

"I will, Mother," Maggie promised, feeling just as lucky as her mother did right now. "Have you given it any more thought about moving into Saltwood Castle with us like Evan offered?"

"I did, and thank you, but I will be living in town instead, with Gertrude and Harold," she answered. "They both got jobs at the alehouse right here in Hythe. I didn't have time to tell you, but I was offered the job of midwife in town, since Gunnora left and it is said she has no intention of returning."

"Oh, Mother, that is wonderful," said Maggie. "Evan

said I will be midwife to everyone in the castle. Mayhap we can even work together sometime like we did in the past."

"I'm sure that will be nice." Her mother pulled out a piece of cloth from a pouch at her side. "Do you remember this?" Unfolding it and holding it up, Maggie saw what it was.

"That is a curtain from our home in Ashenden, isn't it?" asked Maggie. "The one on which you sewed the names of all the babies that you delivered through the years."

"That's right," her mother answered. "I put a new name on here although it is late. Look."

Maggie took the cloth and inspected it. "You added Emma's name to the curtain! Thank you, Mother." She gave it back.

"I was more than happy to finally be able to do it. Gertrude saved the curtains for me years ago while I was in hiding. Lord Ashenden rented our home to another tenant when I disappeared. But Gertrude was able to get the curtains and also save the table and chairs that your father carved for me. We'll be using them in our new home in town."

"Mother, that is wonderful. What a stroke of luck!"

"Yes, I guess so. I suppose I don't need that lucky necklace anymore, after all."

"Neither do I, even though I will keep it," said Maggie. "However, I have another lucky charm now, and that is Evan."

The women all laughed about that.

"Maggie, everyone is waiting," said Evan's mother, sticking her head inside the room.

"I'm ready," said Maggie, thrilled to be marrying Evan,

but nervous, since his father was the Lord Warden of the Cinque Ports and Maggie knew he probably would have wanted his son to marry a noble. Plus, she was going to be meeting all of Evan's relatives today. From what she'd heard there were plenty of them. Supposedly, even his Uncle Storm and his whole crazy family traveled here all the way from Scotland. "Let's go," she said, letting out a deep breath, her hand going to her crystal pendant hanging around her neck. She swore she'd never take this off and never be so careless as to lose it again. After all, she was feeling very lucky in life right now, and she never wanted that to end.

Evan stood at the altar out in the courtyard of Saltwood Castle, waiting for his bride-to-be. Normally, the wedding would take place at church or in the chapel. But since his father liked to do things in big ways, he'd invited half the people in England to the wedding today, and this was the only place big enough to hold all the guests. It wasn't really half of England, but with all of Evan's relatives alone, the place was more than crowded.

"Are you nervous, Cousin?" Daegel asked from the side of his mouth, standing next to Evan. Charles stood next to Daegel at Evan's insistence. The boy was family now. Since Maggie didn't have a lot of family members to join them, Evan wanted to make it special for all of them.

"Why should I be nervous?" Evan whispered back. "You are the next one who will have to get married, so I'd think you'd be more nervous than me."

"Oh." Daegel's expression changed quickly. "I didn't

think of that. Our sisters and cousins will be giving *me* a hard time next, won't they?"

Evan smiled. "Like I said, you have more reason to be nervous than I do."

Evan said the words, but when the minstrels started playing the music and he saw Maggie walking down the aisle, his heart sped up a good amount. Since Maggie didn't have a father, Brother Ruford walked her down the aisle. Little Emma was in front of her throwing petals of roses from a basket as she walked. Her doll Erszba was sitting in the basket as well. Eleanor and Martine were behind Maggie, straightening out her long train.

"God's eyes, she's beautiful," mumbled Evan, his eyes focused on Maggie who looked like an angel or possibly a queen right now. With Eleanor and Martine helping her, Maggie no longer wore the clothes of a commoner or the uniform of a midwife. Today she was dressed like a noble. She wore a blue velvet gown with gold brocade trim. Gold buttons trailed down her arms, leading to the long tippets that hung to the ground. The train of her gown spread out behind her, swishing over the cobblestones as she walked.

Her bright blonde hair was twisted into some kind of knot that wound around her head, topped off by a gold circlet crown. A thin white veil was attached to the head-piece, hanging down her back all the way to her waist. Strands of blonde curls framed her face, not being restricted like the rest of her hair. And in her hands she held a bouquet of pink roses with small white flowers interspersed. Evan had no idea what the white flowers were called, and neither did he care.

All he cared about was the beautiful, amazing woman

with the bright blue eyes whom he once knew as a midwife, but who was now about to be his wife.

The music stopped when Maggie got to the front, and he took her hand as they stood before the priest.

"Family and friends," said the priest. "We are gathered here today for the wedding of Sir Evan Blackmore and Lady Margaret Whitlock."

Maggie's eyes shot over to Evan in alarm. "Evan, you need to tell him I am not a lady," she whispered.

"Shhh," he told her. "Everyone knows. But since you're going to inherit the title once you marry me, it doesn't really matter."

"Oh," said Maggie, letting out a deep sigh. "I'm not sure I'll ever be used to having a courtesy title."

"Just think of it as doing something wild, crazy, and exciting." He smiled at her and winked. She smiled back, and it seemed to help her nervousness.

They said their vows, and then Evan slipped the ring he'd bought onto Maggie's finger.

"It's beautiful!" she gasped, not having seen the ring before now. It was a gold band with etchings of leaves engraved into the gold. Nestled at the top was a big blue sapphire.

"I wanted to get you a stone to match your gorgeous blue eyes," he told her.

"You may kiss the bride," said the priest, and Evan wasted no time in doing so.

The crowd cheered and clapped and the minstrels once again started up with the music.

"We are married now, Maggie," said Evan, as they walked down the aisle, greeting everyone. "Now, I don't want to scare you, but this is my Uncle Storm MacKeefe from Scotland."

"Hello," said Maggie, as Storm stood there with a tankard in his hand.

"Ye are a bonnie lass, Maggie dear," said Storm. "What in the clootie's name are ye doin' marryin' someone like my nephew, Evan?"

"I ... I love him," said Maggie, still sounding overly nervous. Her concerned eyes shot up to Evan.

"Maggie, he's jesting," said Evan.

Storm laughed heartily and slapped Evan on the back. "I didna mean to scare off yer lassie," he told him. "Here, have a tankard of Mountain Magic. Ye look like ye need it." He shoved his drink into Evan's hand.

"I'll take some," said Maggie, reaching for it, but Evan held it to the side.

"You don't even know what's in this tankard," he told her. "It is some of the strongest whisky ever brewed, and not to be taken lightly." Evan raised the tankard to his mouth to take a swig.

"Oh, then I don't want any." Her hand went to her stomach. "I don't think it would be good for our baby."

Evan spit a stream of whisky in the air when he heard this, not realizing that Daegel had walked up, hence getting soaked.

"Are you pregnant, Maggie?" asked Evan.

"Yes. I believe so," she told him.

"Then we have something else to celebrate today. To our baby," Evan called out, raising the tankard high in the air.

"Give me that," griped Daegel, pulling the tankard away from Evan and taking a drink.

"Boys! Dinna waste that whisky by spittin' it all over the place, or ye'll never get me to make more." Storm's grandfather, crazy old Callum MacKeefe, who was known for making Mountain Magic, walked up, waving a bony finger in Daegel's and Evan's faces.

It surprised Daegel and a stream of Mountain Magic shot out of his mouth into the air.

"Ye fool! What did I say about wastin' my whisky?" complained the cantankerous old man.

"Who is that?" Maggie whispered to Evan.

"Oh, you've got a lot to learn about my family, sweetheart," mumbled Evan, pulling Maggie to the side as Callum started going off on one of his tangents. "But that can wait until later. Right now, I want to talk about baby names."

"What?" Maggie giggled.

"Yes, Brother," said Eleanor overhearing and walking up with Martine. "What E name will you be giving your first child?"

"You can use Elrod if it's a boy," suggested Martine. "After all, I told David we will never be using his father's name. Ever."

"Or how about Ella if it's a girl?" asked Eleanor. "Oh, wait. Mayhap not." Her hand went to her stomach. "If I have a girl again, I might want that name, so we'll have to figure this out."

"It doesn't matter to me, what we name our child," said Maggie. "As long as the baby is healthy."

"Then you'd be all right with Erszba, if Emma doesn't mind that we steal her doll's name?" asked Evan.

"Nay," she told him. "Anything but that."

"Well, you'd better start thinking about it," said Evan.

"Since finding six boys' names that start with E might not be easy."

"Evan, please." Maggie looked at him and raised a brow. "I know you are excited but we just got married. We have nine months to think of a name. I don't have one now, because I never thought I'd be pregnant this soon."

"I'm sorry, sweetheart," said Evan, giving Maggie a big, passionate kiss. "I understand about surprises and I welcome excitement and change. You might not have thought you'd be pregnant this soon, but I never even dreamed that I'd one day be **Marrying the Midwife.**"

FROM THE AUTHOR

I hope you enjoyed Evan and Maggie's love story, and that you'll take a moment to leave a review for me. Thank you to all my readers who have been following the *Below the Salt Series,* which is a second-generation romance series about the grown children of my main characters from my *Legacy of the Blade Series*.

If you'd like to read the story of Evan's pirate mother, Echo, you can do so in **Lady of the Mist.** Daegel's father, Lord Corbett's story is found in **Lord of the Blade,** and Storm MacKeefe's story is found in **Lady Renegade.** If you'd like to read about Martine's father, Madoc, and how he raised and raced pigeons when he was a thief, you can do so in **Lord of Illusion.**

You've already met Lady Martine in *Sweet Mead for Lady Martine,* and Lady Eleanor, Evan's sister, in *Dancing on Air*.

This is Book Ten in the series, and yes, there are a few more cousins that need their stories told yet, so keep watching, because you never know when another *Below the Salt* book will appear.

There is a family tree (family up to this point) at the end of this book for your guidance.

Here are the books in the Below the Salt Series up until this point:

Below the Salt Series:

Picking up the Gauntlet – Book 1 (Lady Raven is the daughter of Corbett Blake and Devon from Lord of the Blade.)

A Rose Among Thorns – Book 2 (Lord Rook is Raven's twin brother.)

Love Letters for Lady Lark – Book 3 (Lark is the daughter of Storm MacKeefe and Wren from Lady Renegade.)

Dancing on Air – Book 4 (Lady Eleanor is the daughter of Echo and Garrett Blackmore from Lady of the Mist.)

Winter Sage – Book 5 (Lord Robin is the son of Madoc (Echo's twin brother) and Abbey Blackmore from Lord of Illusion.)

Riding out the Storm – Book 6 (Gar is the son of Echo and stepson/nephew of Garrett from Lady of the Mist.)

Sweet Mead for Lady Martine – Book 7 (Lady Martine is the daughter of Madoc and Abbey from Lord of Illusion.)

Lord of Misrule – Book 8 (Tolin is son of Corbett and Devon from Lord of the Blade.)

Ladybird – Book 9 (Regina is the daughter of Madoc and Abbey from Lord of Illusion.)

<u>Marrying the Midwife</u> – Book 10 (Evan is the son of Echo and Garrett from Lady of the Mist.)

If you'd like to know more about my books, please visit my website at http://elizabethrosenovels.com. You can also follow me on amazon, Facebook, and other social media. Be sure to sign up for my newsletter so you won't miss sales, free books, and new releases. You can do so by going to https://bit.ly/3aK66i2.

Until next time,
Elizabeth Rose

FAMILY TREE

Blake Family Tree:

Evan & Eleanor Blake
   Their children, spouses, their kids, and books where you can read about them:

Corbett married (Devon) – Lord of the Blade
   Rook 'twin' (Primrose Ashdown) – A Rose Among Thorns
   Beowulf
   Raven 'twin' (Jonathon Armstrong) – Picking up the Gauntlet
   Sparrow
   Tolin (Kit Baker)
   Daegel

Wren (Storm MacKeefe) – Lady Renegade
   Renard – Lady Renegade

Lark (Dustin Styles) – Love Letters for Lady Lark
Florie (different father)
Elspeth
Finlay (Seen in Highland Chronicles)
Hawke (Phoebe MacNab) – Highland Storm
Heather (husband)
Liam
(Storm's grandfather is Callum. Storm's parents are Ian & Clarista)

Madoc (Abigail Blackmore) – Lord of Illusion
    Robin (Sage Hillock) – Winter Sage
    Martin
    Martine (David Stone) – Sweet Mead for Lady Martine
    Greta
    William
    Regina (Hunter Chase) – Ladybird
    Dorothy

Echo (Garrett Blackmore) – Lady of the Mist
    Edgar or Gar (different father) (Josefina Waterman) – Riding out the Storm
    Eliot
    Etta (adopted)
    Eleanor (Connor Wyland) – Dancing on Air
    Elizabeth
    Evan (Maggie Whitlock)

Not related - Sorcerer Orrick (Hope Threston) – Keeper of the Flame

ALSO BY ELIZABETH ROSE

Mystery Series:

Harlowe & Fitch Historical Mystery Series

Medieval Series:

Below the Salt

Legendary Bastards of the Crown Series

Seasons of Fortitude Series

Secrets of the Heart Series

Legacy of the Blade Series

Daughters of the Dagger Series

MadMan MacKeefe Series

Barons of the Cinque Ports Series

Holiday Knights Series

Highland Chronicles Series

Pirate Lords Series

Highland Outcasts

Medieval/Paranormal Series:

Elemental Magick Series

Greek Myth Fantasy Series

Tangled Tales Series

Portals of Destiny

Contemporary Series:

Tarnished Saints Series

Working Man Series

Western Series:

Cowboys of the Old West Series

And More!

Please visit http://elizabethrosenovels.com

About Elizabeth

Elizabeth Rose is an award-winning, bestselling author of over 100 books and counting. She writes medieval, historical, contemporary, paranormal, and western romance. Her books are available as EBooks, paperbacks, and some audiobooks as well.

Her favorite characters in her works include dark, dangerous and tortured heroes, and feisty, independent heroines who know how to wield a sword. She loves writing 14th century medieval novels, and is well-known for her many series.

Elizabeth loves the outdoors. In the summertime, you can find her in her secret garden with her laptop, swinging in her hammock working on her next book. Elizabeth is a born storyteller and passionate about sharing her works with her readers.

Please be sure to visit her website at **Elizabethrosenovels.com** to read excerpts from any of her novels and get sneak peeks at covers of upcoming books. You can follow her on **Twitter,** **Facebook**, **Goodreads** or **BookBub.** Join Elizabeth's **newsletter** so you don't miss out on new releases or upcoming events.